Dr. Witherspoon pulled up a chair. "Kidney transplantation is one of the most successful organ transplants we do. And best of all, a person can get along just fine with only one working kidney. That's what makes kidney donation so attractive between relatives. The patient gets a kidney, the donor continues to live a full, active life. Everybody wins."

"But what if you don't have a good match? How successful is it then?"

"With new antirejection drugs, over eighty percent of nonrelated kidneys are still functioning a year later."

Jeremy's heart began to race and his thoughts surged with renewed hope. "Those are good odds."

"Yes." Dr. Witherspoon tipped his head and regarded Jeremy with curiosity. "I assume you have a reason for all this interest in kidney transplants."

Jeremy looked the doctor square in the eye and announced, "Dr. Witherspoon, I want to donate one of my kidneys to Jessica."

SAVING
JESSICA

Lurlene McDaniel

SAVING JESSICA

BANTAM BOOKS
NEW YORK • TORONTO • LONDON • SYDNEY • AUCKLAND

RL 5.2, age 10 and up

SAVING JESSICA

A Bantam Book / May 1996

The Starfire logo is a registered trademark of Bantam Books,
a division of Bantam Doubleday Dell Publishing Group, Inc.
Registered in U.S. Patent and Trademark Office and elsewhere.

ISBN 0-553-56721-7

Published simultaneously in the United States and Canada

Bantam Books are published by Bantam Books, a division of
Bantam Doubleday Dell Publishing Group, Inc. Its trademark,
consisting of the words "Bantam Books" and the portrayal of a
rooster, is Registered in U.S. Patent and Trademark Office and in
other countries. Marca Registrada. Bantam Books, 1540 Broadway,
New York, New York 10036.

PRINTED IN THE UNITED STATES OF AMERICA

OPM   0 9 8 7 6 5 4 3 2 1

To all my loyal readers.
Thank you.

"This is how we know what love is: Jesus Christ laid down his life for us. And we ought to lay down our lives for our brothers. . . . Dear children, let us not love with words or tongue but with actions and in truth." (1 John 3:16 and 18)

SAVING
JESSICA

Chapter

1

"Don't your doctors know *anything* yet? You've been in the hospital two days. You'd think they would have told you *something* by now!"

Jessica McMillan heard the frustration in Jeremy Travino's voice. She held out her hand and he took it, holding it tightly as if he were responsible for keeping her anchored to the hospital bed. "They're supposed to tell me something this afternoon," she told him. "Mom and Dad are coming in at four-thirty for a big powwow with Dr. Kowalski."

"Tell me it won't be bad, Jessie. I don't think I could stand it if something happened to you."

"I'll be all right," she said with much more

assurance than she felt. In truth, she was scared. She'd begun feeling tired and dizzy the month before. *Her* family doctor had treated her for anemia, but her symptoms—headaches, numbness in her arms and legs and an intolerable itching sensation all over her body—had steadily worsened until the doctor had thought it best to hospitalize her and run extensive tests.

"But what if they still don't know anything after all this testing? I've read about weird symptoms that the doctors can't figure out."

"Don't get paranoid on me," she said, peering into Jeremy's worried brown eyes. "Maybe it's something simple—like some kind of exotic flu."

"It's March. Flu season's in the winter."

"So I decided to catch it now. You know how I hate to follow the crowd." She flashed him a smile.

The worry lines in his brow relaxed and he smiled back. "What I know is that I love you and I hate hospitals. What I know is that if they don't let you out of here soon, I'll steal you away from the place."

"My hero," she said with a grin.

He leaned back in the chair beside her bed, still holding her hand. He shrugged sheepishly. "All right, so patience isn't my strong suit. I get it from my father."

Jeremy's dad was a high-powered attorney in a Washington, D.C., firm; his mother was an executive in a public relations business. Jessica's parents were both teachers; her mother helped run a Head Start preschool program and her father taught humanities at Georgetown University.

"Well, since you're a lawyer's son, maybe you should go plead with my doctor to divulge my test results right now and not wait for my parents to arrive."

"I'd do it if I thought he'd talk to us. Why do parents always have to hear everything first?" He sounded irritated.

"Because we're minors?"

"Big deal."

"Don't be impatient. I'm a little scared about hearing the diagnosis anyway. Sometimes *not* knowing can be better than knowing."

"How can you say that? Not knowing is driving me nuts."

"Because as long as I don't know, I can imagine it's something simple, like mono, or anemia that needs more treatment. What if it's something really terrible?"

He moved forward and ran the back of his free hand along her cheek. "No matter what it is, I'll be here for you."

The look of fierce devotion on his face made her insides turn mushy. How had she won the adoration of such a great guy as Jeremy? "Even though I'm an older woman?" she teased.

"Don't start with that. You're not *that* much older."

She was seventeen and a half. He'd turned sixteen in January. But he was so bright and articulate that he seemed older than boys who were eighteen and nineteen. She'd met college-age guys who didn't act as mature as Jeremy.

"Well, most women stop having birthdays at some point, so that'll give you time to catch up to me."

His face broke into a heart-stealing grin. "I like the way that sounds. It sounds as if you plan to have me around for years and years."

"Just until you catch up with me in age. Then I'll have to look for someone younger."

She patted his hand. "You understand, of course."

"Of course. Whatever you say." His dark eyes danced with good humor.

"Hadn't you better get back to school?"

"I want to be with you."

"You've cut two classes and lunch period to be with me. Your parents wouldn't like it if they knew."

His good humor evaporated. "Who cares? I'm tired of them always telling me what to do. They're parents, not my zookeepers."

Jessica wished Jeremy's relationship with his parents was better. They seemed always at odds with each other, always tugging and pulling, prickly as cactuses. Sometimes Jessica thought they resented her relationship with him. She wanted them to like her. She was in love with Jeremy and disliked being the cause of any friction between them and their son. Their only living son.

"Any one of your teachers could tell them you skipped half a day."

"So what? I want to be here when you get your test results. You don't think your folks will mind, do you?"

"No. They won't care if you're with me."
Her parents liked Jeremy and approved of their
dating. Just so long as she graduated in June
and started college in the fall, they would be
happy. Come fall, Jeremy would begin his senior year and she would be attending Georgetown, so she'd be able to see him whenever she
wanted.

"When you get out of here," he said, "I'll
take you to see the cherry trees blossoming
along Pennsylvania Avenue."

"Will you put the top down on your car?"

"We'll freeze."

"We'll turn the heater up and wrap blankets
around us," she countered. She loved his little
sports car, a gift from his parents on his six-
teenth birthday.

"Anything you want." He rubbed his thumb
over her knuckles. "I just want you well again
and out of here."

"Me too." The familiar fear clutched at her.
For a few minutes she'd forgotten where she
was and why, but now reality returned with a
jolt. She was sick. Mysteriously and genuinely
sick. When she'd first protested that she was
fine and didn't want to be checked into the

hospital for testing, her family doctor had said, "Perfectly fine teenage girls don't exhibit such severe symptoms as yours. I want you checked out thoroughly, Jessica."

She'd come to the hospital and spent two days enduring blood tests, X rays and CAT scans. In a few hours she'd know what was wrong. No matter what it was, she hoped she'd have the courage to face it. She squeezed Jeremy's hand. "I'm glad you're here with me. It makes me feel braver."

"I won't leave you," he said. "I promise, I won't."

Her parents arrived at four o'clock, looking tense and worried. They hugged her and told Jeremy they were glad he was there. "Are you feeling all right?" her mother asked anxiously.

"My feet and legs are swollen. I feel like a water balloon."

"You look pretty," her father said.

"I think so too," Jeremy declared.

"I look terrible," she insisted. "And I can't shake this headache."

"Maybe you've got a headache from stress," her mother offered. "I often get stress headaches."

"Maybe so," Jessica said, hoping to calm her mother, who'd been a nervous wreck ever since Jessica had gotten sick. "If it's stress, once I find out what's wrong, the headache will disappear, won't it?"

Her parents looked frightened, and she hated being the cause of their worry. Her father's heart wasn't strong, and her mother had had a bout with breast cancer two years before. She was all right now, but still Jessica worried about their health. It wasn't fair that she should be sick when she should be healthy. Her parents were older—she'd been born late in their lives—but they adored her. She was their only child.

"How have you been, Jeremy?" her father asked.

"Okay. I'll be better when Jessie's home." He gazed at her tenderly and she smiled.

"We all will."

The doctor was late. "Maybe I should have the nurses page him," her mother said. "What do you think, Don?"

"He'll be here, Ruth. You know doctors. Always with a million things to do."

Jessica felt the tension in the room and wished she could do something to lessen it. But she was feeling slightly nauseous and couldn't think of anything to say to her parents.

Jeremy turned on the TV and found the CNN channel. The newscaster's voice droned, but it was enough to grab everyone's attention. Jessica told Jeremy "Thank you" with her eyes. Finally, at five-fifteen, Dr. Kowalski breezed into the room along with Dr. Harris, the family physician. Their faces were masklike and unreadable, but Jessica felt a stab of fear. If only they'd been smiling.

"I think we've got a diagnosis," Dr. Kowalski said, getting right to the point. "I asked Dr. Harris along because he was able to help figure out the *how* that went along with the *why.*"

"What are you talking about?" Jessica's father asked.

Dr. Kowalski set a thick file folder on the tray table over Jessica's bed. He looked straight at her. "You're in kidney failure, Jessica. Your symptoms could fit the profile of many diseases and medical problems, but the itchiness was the clue that led me to suspect your kidneys weren't functioning properly."

"My kidneys?"

"It isn't cancer?" her mother blurted.

"No," Dr. Kowalski said.

Her mother was so relieved that she sagged.

The two doctors turned their attention to Jessica. Dr. Harris picked up her hand and held it gently between his palms. "You're in end-stage renal disease," he told her quietly. "Total kidney failure."

"But people can't live without kidneys," Jeremy said, coming up beside her bed and locking eyes with the doctor.

"You'll have to begin dialysis immediately," the doctor continued, turning his attention back to Jessica. "It will take over the function of your kidneys and keep you alive."

Chapter

2

"Kidney failure! But how is that possible?" Jessica felt as incredulous as her father. With her heart pounding and her mouth as dry as cotton, she waited for the doctors to answer his question.

"That's what I wanted to know," Dr. Harris told them. "When Dr. Kowalski called with the results of your lab work, I went back through all your files. You've been my patient since you were a newborn, and your family's given you the best of care." He paused to nod toward her mother and father.

"Two years ago, I treated you for a strep infection—but not until it was pretty advanced. Whether you know it or not, untreated strep can cause a host of problems, including rheumatic fever, which affects the heart. In your case, I believe it took a toll on your kidneys. The damage progressed slowly and relentlessly until you were so far along that now there's nothing we can do about it. Except put you on dialysis."

Jessica's head was spinning. This couldn't be happening to her! How had something gotten so serious with so little warning?

Dr. Kowalski added, "The point is you're in kidney failure, Jessica, and that's what we have to deal with."

"How are 'we' going to do that?" Her voice was barely a whisper.

"You're getting a new doctor. My colleague Ronald Witherspoon is a top-notch nephrologist—that's a specialist in the treatment of kidney disorders. He'll be in shortly to explain your course of treatment. He'll put you on a hemodialysis machine, which will do the work of your kidneys and make you feel a whole lot better. Your edema will clear up, as will the headaches and itching. You'll feel good again in no time."

The news was so devastating that she couldn't imagine ever feeling good again. Certainly not emotionally, anyway. Her body had turned on her, betrayed her, destroyed her kidneys, and her life would never be the same.

"H-How long will Jessie be on this dialysis?" her mother asked. Her face was ashen and pinched, and suddenly she looked much older than her fifty-five years.

"For as long as she lives," Dr. Kowalski said quietly. "Her kidneys won't regenerate."

My whole life! A wave of nausea swept through Jessica.

"Three days a week you'll come to the dialysis center and be placed on a dialysis machine. The machine takes over the function of your kidneys, cleanses your blood of wastes and toxins, adjusts your body fluids and balances blood chemicals. Unfortunately, it can't replace the hormone that aids in making red blood cells, so we'll have to treat your anemia with medication."

She didn't care about how the process worked. She only wanted to wake up from this terrible nightmare.

"Is being hooked up to this machine the only way you can help Jessie?" Jeremy asked. She held on to his hand as if it were a lifeline.

"There's always transplantation," the doctor said. "But finding a donor isn't always easy. Many factors have to be weighed, but kidney transplants are our most successful area of transplantation if you become a candidate for one."

He made it sound like an election. "Do I have a choice?" she asked.

Dr. Harris patted her arm. "Dr. Witherspoon will be better able to discuss the next phase of your treatment with you. Write down all your questions for him." He peered down at her through steel-rimmed glasses; his eyes seemed clouded and misty. "I'm sorry, Jessica. So very, very sorry."

When both doctors had gone, she began to cry. Her parents wept with her, holding her, soothing her as if she were once again a tiny child. Only Jeremy remained dry-eyed, but when he took her in his arms she could feel the tension in his muscles, the fierceness in his grip as he crushed her against him. "You'll lick this thing, Jessie," he whispered. "You will."

"How can I? Didn't you hear them? It's incurable. I don't want to be hooked up to a machine for the rest of my life. How can I have a life when I need a machine to help me live?" She sobbed until there were no more tears left in her. Jeremy continued to hold her.

Finally her father spoke. "I know this is horrible, honey, but it's not the end of the world. You *are* alive. Mom and I will help you however we can. The first thing to do is read up on it. Find out all we can."

She knew it was her father's way. He tackled life's problems armed with as much knowledge as possible. He'd raised her to believe that fear was the true enemy and that knowledge did much to banish fear.

"I'll quit my job," her mother announced. "I want to take care of you."

In spite of her grief, Jessica felt a twinge of guilt. She didn't want her parents sacrificing themselves on her account. "Mom, please don't do anything drastic yet."

"But you'll have to go to dialysis three days a week. I can't let you go alone."

"I'll drive her," Jeremy said quietly.

"She's our daughter," Ruth said.

Jessica disliked having them discuss her as if she weren't even there. "I might be able to drive myself, you know," she said. "I'm sure if this is something that I'll have to do the rest of my life, I'll have to manage on my own eventually."

The conversation stopped abruptly when Dr. Witherspoon entered the room. He was a short, balding man with expressive brown eyes. After introductions, he explained more about the different kinds of dialysis. Jessica felt a glimmer of hope when he told them that sometimes dialysis could be done at a patient's home, on a smaller dialysis machine, and could be done at night while the patient slept.

But her hopes were dashed when he said that at first, and "for a while," she would go to a treatment center near the McMillans' home in Reston, Virginia, a suburb of Washington. He told her that early the next morning she'd undergo a minor surgical procedure to create a fistula under the skin of the inside of her left arm.

"I'll join together one of your veins to one of your arteries, and in a short time the vein will enlarge and strengthen. This makes it easier to insert the two needles of the dialysis machine. In the meantime, we'll prepare an external shunt, which does the same thing but shows more on the outside of your arm. A nurse will cap off the special tubing after each treatment and bandage your arm."

Jessica gulped. "Do I have to have the needles stuck in me every time I go for dialysis?"

"Yes. It won't be so bad," he said, patting her arm. "The nurse will numb your arm before inserting the needles. Then you'll be attached to the dialyzer, and your blood will be cleansed and pumped back into your body. The cleaning process doesn't hurt, and while you're being dialyzed you can read, watch TV, talk on the phone, do homework."

"I'll look like a freak!" Jessica didn't like the idea one bit.

"The fistula is under the skin; no one can see it. However, it's very important that you take good care of the site regardless of the type of access device we use. I don't want it to become infected or have a blood clot form. Don't worry, you'll get plenty of information about proper care. And, of course, you'll be going in for treatments often, and the staff will keep a watchful eye out for problems."

"Our daughter will be all right, won't she?" Jessica heard the edge of hysteria in her father's voice.

"As long as she remains on dialysis, she'll be able to lead a fairly normal life."

Normal! Jessica almost laughed in his face.

Dr. Witherspoon must have caught her expression because he added, "As normal as possible anyway. You're going to be bombarded with information over the next few days," he added. "It may seem overwhelming at first. You'll have to go on a special low-potassium diet. You'll have to be treated for anemia, maybe high blood pressure. You run the risk of hepatitis, bone deterioration, neuropathy— that's nerve damage."

"You're scaring us," her father said.

"I want you to understand how serious your daughter's condition is."

Jessica felt numb with the understanding.

"You can't miss dialysis treatments." Dr. Witherspoon looked directly at her. "I know you're young, and I know how devastating this news is for you. But you can't ignore your disease, or mistreat your body. Renal failure once was an automatic death sentence. But today, with dialysis, kidney patients can have long, productive lives."

"And a transplant? What about a transplant?" Jessica knew no machine could truly take the place of a living, working organ, so she was interested in that option.

"This hospital has one of the best transplant facilities in the country, so that is a possibility. But that path isn't an easy one. For starters, thousands of people are waiting for kidneys. There's a waiting list and a sophisticated system of selection." He folded her chart, glanced at his watch and prepared to leave.

"I know you have other questions. I'll send in some of my support staff, who will bring you literature, videotapes, books. A dietician will be in to see you too. And tomorrow morning I'll insert that shunt. It'll take a few days for the internal connection to strengthen before it can be used. In the meantime, we'll begin dialysis while you're here. You will get through this, Jessica. I promise."

Alone in the room with her parents and Jeremy, she glanced helplessly from face to face. "Why is this happening to me?"

No one had an answer. Her parents looked so devastated, she wasn't sure they could drive themselves home. But the look of sheer determination on Jeremy's face was the one that gave her strength and courage. "We'll get through this," he said.

She nodded. "I suppose I will."

"And I'll be here with you every day."

She wanted to believe him more than anything. But she was the one who was sick, and he had a year and a half of high school ahead of him. How long before he grew tired of having a sick girlfriend? A girlfriend who would be committed to a thrice-weekly rendezvous with a machine that kept her alive?

Chapter
3

Jeremy drove to his house much too fast. He was risking getting a speeding ticket, and if he got one his father would have a fit, but Jeremy didn't care. He couldn't think of anything except his beloved Jessie and the ordeal she was facing.

"It isn't fair!" he shouted. The wind rushing through the open car windows snatched his voice away. Icy March air made his face numb, but he didn't care about that either. He was beyond caring about his own physical comfort. All he knew was that Jessica was sick. That she might be taken away from him. The way Tom had been.

He came to a screeching halt in the driveway

of the Tudor-style brick house in an upscale Reston neighborhood, bolted from the car and ran inside. He was late for dinner. His parents were sitting in the dining room. It was a rare weeknight that his father was home. Startled, they looked up as Jeremy careened into the room, dragged his chair across the polished oak floor and lush oriental carpet and settled in a heap.

"Good heavens!" his father snapped. "Mind your manners. This isn't a barn, you know."

"What's wrong?" his mother asked. As usual, she was the more perceptive of the two.

"Jessica's in kidney failure." Jeremy's voice fairly shook with emotion. "She starts dialysis tomorrow."

"Oh, no!" His mother rose and came to put her arm around his shoulders. "Jeremy, I'm so sorry. Tell us everything."

Briefly he told them.

"Poor Jessie," his mother said, glancing over to her husband, who sat tight-lipped and wordless. "And her poor parents. Is there anything we can do?"

"There's nothing anybody can do. Nothing. But I know I want to be there for her."

His father broke his silence. "How do you mean?"

"Once she gets on a schedule, I want to help take her for her treatments so that her mother won't have to quit her job. I want to be around her, help any way I can."

His parents exchanged glances. "What about your own life? Your schoolwork?" his father asked.

"How can you even ask such a dumb question?" Jeremy asked, leaping up.

"I resent your attitude—"

Jeremy's mother interrupted. "Frank, he's had a terrible shock. I don't think now's the time for the two of you to start arguing."

Frank Travino threw up his hands. "You're right, Marilyn." He took a deep breath. "I am sorry about Jessica, son. Go ahead and spend as much time as you need to until she gets situated. Just don't forget that you have a responsibility to live your own life."

Jeremy wanted to announce that Jessica *was*

his life, but thought better of it. "I'm going up to my room," he said.

"Eat some dinner," his mother urged.

"I'm not hungry." She looked distraught, so he added, "Maybe later."

He went up the spiral staircase to his room, where he leaned heavily against the closed door trying to sort through his emotions. His room was spacious, with a computer, bookcases, a TV and audio equipment taking up one entire wall. A weight-lifting bench stretched along another.

A bulletin board over his desk was crammed with a jumble of photos of Jessica and himself. Slowly he walked over to study the pictures. There were photos of them together out at his family's lake home the previous summer. Pictures of them at three high-school dances, and more recent ones from Christmas. In every one, Jessica looked radiant, beautifully infused with life and exuberance.

A sob knotted his throat, but he refused to let it out. He hadn't cried since his brother Tom's funeral, three years earlier. Jessica was alive and under good medical care. She was going to be all right. She *had* to be! He picked up the phone and dialed the hospital. Jessica picked up on the third ring.

"How are you?" he asked.

"All cried out," she told him. "They fed me supper and I can't eat again after midnight."

"When's your surgery?"

"Seven in the morning."

"I'll be there."

"It's minor, Jeremy. You should go to school. Come visit in the afternoon."

"No way."

"You can't keep skipping classes."

"I'm a genius, remember?" His IQ was sky-high. He'd skipped a grade when he was younger and could have skipped another, but hadn't wanted to start college at sixteen. He asked, "Don't you want me there when you wake up?"

"Of course I do. It made a world of difference that you were here today when I got the bad news. My parents mean well, but they want to put me in a plastic bubble."

He understood completely. Ever since Tom's death, his parents had been hyperprotective of him too. And his father kept pressuring him to study and do well. He guessed he was expected to take over his brother's life role. "I told my parents about all you're going through, and they're really sorry. I don't think they'll hassle me over any time I spend with you."

"I—I really want you with me," Jessica confessed.

He felt a rush of protectiveness and wished he had the power to change what was happening to her. "You saved my life, Jessie. I want to help however I can."

When they'd first met the year before, when he was just fifteen, he'd had recurring thoughts of dying. He hadn't been able to stop thinking about the accident that had killed his brother. Even now the memory was vivid, a kaleidoscope of crystal-clear impressions: his older brother, Tom, a new cadet at Annapolis, home for the weekend. Riding with Tom to the movie. The wet road. The long skid. Tom turning the car to take the impact of a tree on his side of the car. Tom had died instantly; thirteen-year-old Jeremy had walked away with barely a scratch.

I should have been the one to die, he thought. Jessica was the only person he'd ever told how he felt. Because he was so smart, the high school had placed him in an advanced English class, and that's where he'd met Jessica. She was friendly, pretty and easy to talk to. It didn't take him long to fall for her. And to explore with her his pent-up feelings about his brother's death. They'd had long talks, far into the night when they were studying together, and slowly, haltingly, he'd opened up his heart to her.

"God doesn't make mistakes," she'd told him at the time. "You've been saved for a purpose. Maybe you should find out what it is."

"I didn't 'save your life,' " she told him over the phone. "You just needed someone to talk to. I think you're the most interesting guy I've ever met. I care about you."

He knew she'd taken a lot of flak from her friends when she started dating a guy a year and a half younger, but she'd ignored them. He said, "I like being around you too."

"Even if you can't take me out to eat anymore?"

"What do you mean?"

"The dietician gave me some bad news."

"Tell me."

"The diet is the pits. No bananas. No orange

juice. And my love affair with potatoes is all but over."

"No potatoes either?" He knew how much she loved french fries and potato chips.

"I have to watch everything I put into my mouth—even water has to be monitored. I don't see how I can live this way."

He heard a catch in her voice and longed to reach through the phone and hold her. "Okay, so you have to juggle your diet. We'll do it. And if you can't eat certain stuff, then I won't either."

"You can't do that."

"Says who? I can eat whatever I want."

"Because I don't want you to," Jessica said. "I don't want your life to get turned upside down too."

"All right—then I won't eat your favorite foods in front of you." He desperately wanted to make her laugh. "And if we get served something you can't eat, I'll stuff it in my socks right there at the table."

"My hero."

He heard the hint of a smile. "Remember the long talks we used to have? When I was still so messed up about Tom?"

"I remember."

"You told me that no matter how bad things got in life, if I'd just wait them out, life would get better again. It was hard to believe. But you were right, Jessie. Things have gotten better again, even though Tom's not ever coming home."

"I hate it when you give me back my own advice," she said with a sigh. "Even when I know you're right. I know it could be so much worse. . . . I could need a new heart, or liver. There are no machines to fill in for those organs. I just don't like the whole idea. It's scary. To be hooked to a machine for . . . for maybe the rest of my life. What kind of life is that, Jeremy?"

He couldn't answer her because he thought the idea appalling also. "You'll make it," he said fiercely. "You have to."

"Why? What makes me different from the thousands of people already in dialysis?"

"Because I love you. And I won't lose you, Jessie. I won't."

Chapter

4

Jessica stared glumly at the tube snaking from the inside of her forearm resting on the recliner-style chair to the machine next to her. The compact dialyzer hummed, doing the work of her now-defunct kidneys. It cleansed her blood of wastes and toxins and returned it to her body purified and ready to begin the cycle of cellular waste removal all over again. She had been on dialysis for seven weeks now —three times a week, four hours a day. And she hated it.

"You look sad, Jessica."

The nurse's statement intruded on Jessica's dark thoughts. She sighed. "Do you realize that I see more of this machine than I do my friends and family?"

The nurse, Pat, pulled up a stool next to Jessica's recliner. "I know how limiting this can be for a girl your age. Most people who come here are elderly or diabetic."

The dialysis unit was a large room with about twenty recliners and dialysis machines. Nurses and social workers made their way down the aisles, visiting with patients, checking lines and medication flows, attending to those unable to leave the confines of the chair during the dialysis process. TV sets were suspended from the ceilings, and most people watched the afternoon soap operas and game shows. Jessica was the only person under the age of fifty, and she felt like a freak and a foreigner.

She turned toward Pat, being careful to keep her arm steady. "I still throw up after most sessions. And the headaches are awful. Dialysis isn't making me feel as good as the doctors said it would."

"Sometimes it takes a while to work out a balance."

Dr. Witherspoon had changed mixes and medications several times already. Jessica took a fistful of prescription pills, plus vitamins, measured every morsel she ate, and still had problems. "Well, at least I've learned to knit. I've been knitting a ski cap that's five feet long for Jeremy's Christmas present and it's only May. Imagine how long it'll be by December twenty-fifth."

Pat smiled. "A positive attitude really helps, you know."

"Well, as they say around here—consider the alternative." Jessica studied Pat, then asked, "Have you known many patients who got transplants?"

"Several. A few drop by now and again to say hello."

Jessica had been thinking about transplantation more and more, and the idea both attracted and frightened her. While it would be wonderful to be free of the machine, it was scary to contemplate a life with the ever-present threat of rejection. She asked, "What if I did get a transplant, and then it rejected on me?"

"Then you'd go back on dialysis until we found you another kidney."

Jessica couldn't imagine getting to live like a regular person again, then having to return to dialysis. It seemed terribly cruel. How many chances would the doctors give her? How many kidneys would they allow her?

"So, how's Jeremy?" Pat changed the subject. "Is he taking you to your prom? My daughter's been looking for just the right dress for her prom for a month, and she's not even been asked yet!"

Jessica was glad to shift her thoughts to her favorite topic—Jeremy. "No prom for me. I really don't want to go."

"But you're a senior. You should go."

"You sound like my mother. But I get the cold shivers when I think about having to find a dress that covers my arms, or picking a restaurant and having to think about every bite I put in my mouth, or getting sick right in the middle and having to rush home."

"Where there's a will, there's a way."

"No will, no way," she confessed.

"Still, it's only one night," Pat said. "I'll bet you could make it."

"Proms aren't simple little dances anymore. Around here they're two- and three-day marathon parties. Kids move from party to party, even from city to city. One guy in our senior class has parents who own a horse farm, and he's invited a third of the class there for picnicking and riding all weekend. Another friend's father owns a boat, and she's having a gang come for an overnighter on the Potomac."

"Gee, what ever happened to simplicity?"

"It's passé." Jessica looked up to see Jeremy walking down the rows of recliners toward her. As always, her heartbeat accelerated. He meant so much to her, and she regretted that his life had changed because hers had. She wondered often why he hadn't started looking for another girlfriend.

"Am I early?" he asked, dipping down to kiss her lightly on the lips.

"No, Boris and I are about through for the day." She motioned toward the blue-and-white machine that shuttled her blood back and forth. "He's made me squeaky clean again, and I don't have to look at his smiling face for two whole days. That's the best part about Fridays." Her routine was to come every other day after school, with weekends off. Except on Mondays, when she arrived at six in the morning so that she could dialyze before school. But after a weekend away from dialysis, she was sick and puffy with water weight and built-up toxins.

Jeremy waited while Pat unhooked Jessica and bandaged her arm. "We'll see you Monday morning," he said to Pat when they were ready to leave.

Outside in the bright sunlight, Jessica sucked in the fresh air to drive out the medicine smell of the dialysis unit. Sometimes she felt as if the odor clung to her body permanently and no amount of bathing could wash it away. She drenched herself in cologne daily.

Jeremy pulled out of the parking lot and merged into the fast-moving traffic, heading toward her house. "You up to a movie tonight?"

"Maybe. I'm feeling a little light-headed. All this clean blood, I guess." She leaned her head against the seat, fighting down nausea.

Concerned, Jeremy glanced over at her. She looked pale, and his stomach constricted. He'd thought that dialysis would make her well again, but it hadn't. She still had many days when she could barely function. She tried her best to hide it when she felt sick, but he could always tell when she was faking it. "You want to stop for a snack? Maybe you need to eat something."

"Eating isn't much fun anymore. Too many restrictions."

"How about something to drink?"

"Same thing." She had to measure every ounce of liquid. If she drank too much fluid, it built up, put pressure on her lungs and made it harder for her to breathe. "Look on the bright side. Since I don't drink much fluid, I don't go to the bathroom very often." She patted his hand. "Now isn't *that* a bonus? No more waiting on me while I go to the ladies' room at the movies or the mall."

"I'd wait for you outside a bathroom for three days if you could be well again."

She felt a headache beginning to build, leaned her head against his shoulder and mumbled, "If only."

At her house, Jessica's mother insisted that she lay down until suppertime. She helped Jessica up the staircase while Jeremy stood at the bottom and watched helplessly. He would have traded places with her if he could.

"Stay for dinner," Jessica called down to him

from the top of the stairs. "After supper, if I feel better, I'd like to go to that movie with you."

Her mother added, "Yes, please stay, Jeremy. Go on in the kitchen. I'll be there as soon as I get Jessie settled in."

He wanted to stay. He wanted to be with Jessica. His father was working late and that morning his mother had driven up to New York for a couple of days on business. Going home and being alone didn't appeal to him at all. He went into the roomy kitchen and settled on a bar stool at the counter.

The kitchen island was piled with scrubbed vegetables and the makings of a salad. Roasting meat and freshly baked bread smelled delicious and made his stomach growl. On one wall there was an elaborate chart detailing the foods and their nutritional content along with the levels of calories, protein, sodium, potassium, calcium and phosphorus that a kidney patient could eat. Next to the chart was a memo board with a special pen where Jessica's mother planned out every meal, factoring in the amounts of each nutrient Jessica had to have in exact proportions. It looked complicated and reminded him again of the difficult course her life had taken.

Ruth McMillan breezed into the kitchen. "She's resting, but she made me promise to wake her in an hour." Her brow furrowed. "She wants you to be here when she gets up. Can you stay?"

"I can stay."

Ruth looked preoccupied.

Jeremy said, "I thought dialysis would make her better."

"She is better."

"But she's not *as* better as I figured she'd be."

Ruth looked up from her work with the food, her eyes dark with concern. Jeremy's heart thudded, then accelerated its pace. "What's wrong, Mrs. McMillan? I know something's wrong."

Her gaze flitted away, but he could tell she wanted to tell him what was on her mind. "You're right—Jessica isn't doing as well as she should be. She isn't doing very well at all."

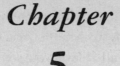

Chapter
5

"How do you mean?" Jeremy pushed off the stool and walked around the island to face her.

"According to her latest blood work, her blood urea nitrogen, or BUN, level is still too high, and when dialysis brings it down, she gets nauseous and throws up. Even though I make sure she eats right, her BUN won't cooperate."

His mind worked rapidly, sorting through what Ruth was telling him. BUN tests measured the level of waste products in Jessica's bloodstream. "Are you saying that dialysis isn't helping her?"

"Oh, it's helping. It's just not helping

enough." She looked into Jeremy's eyes again. "She is sticking to her diet, isn't she? I mean, at school and all. Have you seen her cheat by eating something she shouldn't?"

Even if he had, he wouldn't have told on Jessica, but he could honestly say, "I've never seen her cheat."

"Dr. Witherspoon's concerned. He wants us to think seriously about a transplant."

Jeremy froze. "That's heavy."

Ruth shook her head. "Her father and I are scared about it, but I think Jessica wants one."

Jessica hadn't spoken to him about it, and that hurt his feelings. He'd thought they talked about everything. "Wouldn't a transplant make her well?" He longed for her to be free of the dialysis machine.

"If a new kidney takes, she'll be much better off. No more dialysis. But a lifetime of anti-rejection drugs. Still, the trade-off seems to be worth it."

Jeremy thought so too. He knew how much Jessica hated the machine and the way it limited and controlled her life. "There are other kinds of dialysis," he said. "I've read about the kind they do through a tube in the abdomen."

The idea made him shudder, but he didn't let on to Jessica's mother. "And it can be done at home."

"Yes, peritoneal dialysis. But she'd have to wear a bag under her clothes filled with the dialysis fluid."

"That sounds grim."

"It would be. But her doctor doesn't feel she's a candidate for that kind of dialysis. Of course, we can try it and get her a home dialysis unit so she can dialyze during the night. But that doesn't seem like much of a solution to me either."

"Which brings us back to a transplant."

"Yes. Aside from it being major surgery, there are thousands of people waiting for kidney transplants. There just aren't enough donor organs to go around."

His hopes for Jessica plummeted. "Then why would he bring it up?"

"Because he thinks it's her best hope. She's a young girl with her whole life ahead of her. She wants to go to college and have a career. A transplant now would give her a chance at a more normal life."

He weighed the information, seeing it as a

complicated problem worthy of his most dedicated study. "Where can she get a kidney?"

"Of course there are cadaver kidneys—donated from dead people—but Dr. Witherspoon says she's not a candidate for one of those. Something to do with antibodies already built up in her system." She waved her hand. "I don't pretend to understand it all. Anyway, he told us that the best transplant donors are live related ones. Like members of a person's own family. Her father and I would gladly give her one of our kidneys." She glanced around the kitchen as if someone might be listening in. "We don't want Jessica to know it yet, but the doctor is running an antigen match on us."

"What's an antigen match?"

"The closer the tissues match, the better the chance that the organ won't be rejected. If an identical twin gives a kidney to his or her sibling, the match is ideal."

"But Jessica's not a twin. And she hasn't got any brothers or sisters."

"True. Her closest blood relative is a cousin, my sister's son, but he's grown and married with a family of his own to take care of. We can't ask him to volunteer." She shook her head. "I just hope one of us is a good match for her."

Jeremy considered what she'd told him as she hurried to turn off the oven timer, which had begun to buzz loudly. He imagined Jessica back to a regular life with a transplanted kidney. If it happened soon enough, she might be able to start college in the fall as she'd originally planned. A transplant would put this nightmare behind all of them. Jessie would have her life back, and he would have his Jessie back. It made sense to him that a transplant was the way to go.

He glanced up at the kitchen clock. "It's been about an hour since Jessie lay down."

"Maybe I should let her sleep."

"She wouldn't like it. You know how she hates to feel babied."

Ruth sighed. "Oh, all right."

"Can I go up and wake her?"

Ruth smiled. "She'd appreciate seeing your face more than mine, I guess."

He grinned, then left the kitchen, bounded up the staircase and down the hall to Jessica's room. He knocked lightly, then eased open the door. The shades over the windows were pulled, darkening the room. Gauzy, flowing curtains pooled on the carpeted floor.

He thought Jessica's bedroom reflected her perfectly. It was feminine and pretty, scented like summer flowers and fresh spring rain, softened with colors of May—lavender and white peppered with daffodil yellow. There were bookcases, a table with two white wicker chairs and a Queen Anne–style desk that held a computer. The incongruity of technology and romanticism sitting side by side made him smile. He couldn't imagine this room filled with a dialysis machine and bags of fluid, and smelling of medicine.

Jessica lay on her bed, her hair spilling across her pillow. He stared down at her, caressing her with his gaze. She looked pale, yet beautiful. Her thick, dark lashes almost brushed her cheeks. He wanted to kiss her rosebud-shaped mouth.

Jeremy dropped to his knees beside her bed and tenderly stroked her forehead. She made a sound, but didn't wake. Unable to resist, he leaned forward and ever so softly pressed his lips to hers. Then he laid his cheek on the pillow, close to her face, until their noses were almost touching.

Her eyes opened slowly, focusing on his face. She smiled. "Hi."

"Hi, princess."

"Are you my Prince Charming waking me from the spell of some wicked witch?"

"Fooled you. I'm really a frog in disguise."

She touched his cheek. "Some frog."

He wanted to crawl beneath the covers with her, hold her body against his and never let her go. "Have I told you today that I love you?"

"I can't remember. Better tell me again."

"I love you."

Her eyes, large and the color of blue sky, studied him seriously. "Even though I'm broken?"

He reared back. "You're not broken. You've got a health problem. But it doesn't change *who* you are. And it doesn't change the way I feel about you."

She propped her back against the headboard. Her hair was disheveled, and she still wore the pale pink sweater from that afternoon. He thought she looked delectable. Like cotton candy. He sat on the edge of the bed and took her hands in his. "I've been talking to your mother. She says you've been thinking about a kidney transplant. Why didn't you say something to me about it?"

"I was going to. I've been reading up on it." She turned toward the window. In spite of the shade's being drawn, she gave the impression that she was looking at the tree outside her window. "Kidneys are living things. If I ever get one, I'll take very good care of it."

"You should get one. You deserve one."

She cupped the side of his face in her hand. "I'm one of thousands needing a kidney. I have type O blood—the most common kind. That puts me even farther down on the transplant list because there are so many people with O blood type—rarer blood types often get higher priority than us garden-variety types."

"You're *not* garden-variety."

She shushed him with a glance. "And I haven't been on dialysis very long either, which is another disadvantage. Those who've been on the longest and who have the greatest need get first consideration."

He saw the complexity of the issue. "But your mother said that if you have a live related donor, you wouldn't have to go on the donor waiting list."

Jessica shook her head. "I don't have many relatives. I know that my parents want to be considered as potential donors because I saw them look at each other when Dr. Witherspoon was discussing it, but even if they're a match, they've both had serious health problems."

"So?"

"So, they're ineligible."

Her statement caught him up short. "Your mother doesn't think so."

"She doesn't know yet." Jessica gestured toward her desk, where pamphlets and books lay open. "Did you know that a kidney from a sixty-year-old transplanted into a twenty-year-old ceases to age? It's true. Why, it can function for years and years." Her expression clouded. "Provided it doesn't reject, that is."

"Are you afraid if you got one it would reject?"

She nodded. "I've had bad dreams about it. I see myself running in a field and just when I think I'm free, I notice this long plastic tube attached to my side. I wake up in a cold sweat, terrified I'll never be rid of the machine."

He took her in his arms, wishing he could chase away her demon fears. "If you reject, you reject. They'll find you another kidney."

"That's what Pat at the dialysis unit said." Jessica laughed without humor. "As if they grow on trees and you can run right out and pick one."

"You're not giving up on getting a transplant already, are you?"

"Of course not. But I have to be realistic, Jeremy. People don't always get what they want." She leaned forward and kissed him deeply. "Not even princesses," she added softly.

Chapter
6

When Jeremy arrived home that night, his father was in his study poring over law books.

"Big case?" Jeremy asked, standing in the doorway.

His father sighed, taking off his glasses and pinching the bridge of his nose between his thumb and forefinger. "Yes. I have to go before a federal judge next month."

Jeremy knew enough about his father's profession to understand that federal cases were often more complicated than state cases because they sometimes set legal precedents. "Good luck."

The house seemed too quiet, especially after the sociability of the dinner table at Jessica's, where everybody talked with one another. He and Jessica had decided against the movie, so he'd driven around aimlessly for a while before coming home. Now, seeing his father hunched over his work and realizing his mother wouldn't be home until later tomorrow, Jeremy felt at loose ends. Purposeless. Although he and his father often grated on each other's nerves, he felt pangs of nostalgia, remembering better days when he and Tom and his dad did fun things together and never fought.

His father must have sensed Jeremy's hesitation to leave because he pushed back from his desk and gestured toward the couch. "Sit down and visit."

"I don't want to interrupt."

"You're my son. It's not an interruption."

Jeremy settled on the leather couch, stretching out his long legs and clasping his hands behind his head.

"How's Jessica?"

Briefly Jeremy discussed her problems and her hope of a transplant and finished by saying, "I'm sure she'd have a transplant if there were a donor available."

"Makes sense to me. She's so young; it seems

a shame to commit her to a lifetime of dialysis when a transplant could set her free."

Jeremy appreciated his father's sympathetic tone, for although he didn't hassle him, Jeremy knew his father wasn't thrilled about the amount of time he spent with Jessica. "I'd sure like to see her get one hundred percent again," said Jeremy. "I miss doing things with her. I don't like that her kidney disease takes up so much of our time together. That sounds selfish, doesn't it?"

"No. When you care about somebody, you want the best for them."

"I really like her, you know." Jeremy wanted to say he loved her, but felt the word might be too strong and put his father off.

"I know. She's a lovely girl."

"You and Mom approve of her?"

His father looked puzzled. "Sure. When I look around and see what some kids bring home—friends with blue hair, earrings in their noses, studded leather clothes—yes, I think Jessica is a fine choice."

Jeremy grinned, warming to his father's affable mood. "Then I guess I shouldn't ask to get my belly button pierced."

His father grimaced. "Just thinking about it makes me cringe."

"Didn't you ever do something that went against the mainstream when you were growing up?"

"Are you kidding? In law school I had hair down to my shoulders."

"No lie?" Jeremy couldn't imagine his father's close-cropped brown hair so long.

"And I once organized a revolt against the curfew in the dorms. A group of us camped out in front of the dean's office door for a week. We were loud, smelly and obnoxious. We really disrupted his life—all campus life, in fact. The campus newspaper and local TV station covered our cause and turned us into minicelebrities."

"Did you win?"

"'Course not. My father called and told me if I didn't straighten out, he'd cut off my funds and I'd have to drop out of law school."

"And you gave in?" Jeremy felt a twinge of disappointment.

"I had always believed that the ends justified the means, but a person has to know when to cut his losses and bow out gracefully. Besides, I wanted that law degree."

"Does Mom know you had this wild side?"

"Who do you think brought us our meals during our sit-in?"

Jeremy laughed aloud over the image of his very proper parents acting totally antisocial. "Did it blow over?"

"Actually, the university pressed charges and I had to be my own defense attorney."

"You could do that before you became a lawyer?"

"Sure. The courts allow senior law students to take on cases if the student practices under the supervision of a law professor."

Jeremy leaned forward, eager to hear the outcome of his father's story. "So what happened when you went to court?"

"I did a good enough job to get us all off with a fine and community service. We could have been expelled."

"And you like practicing law, don't you?"

"I always have. Discovering the weakness in my opponent's case, outsmarting my opponent, winning—it still gives me a rush." His father leaned back in his swivel chair. "You think you might be interested in law?"

"I'm not sure."

His father picked up a pencil and tapped it on the arm of the chair. "Listen, I was going to ask this later, but now seems like a good time. How'd you like to be a clerk at the firm this summer? Pay's above minimum wage and the work's interesting."

Jeremy immediately thought about his time with Jessica. "I told Jessica's parents I'd help drive her to dialysis. And . . . and I want to spend as much time as I can with her."

"We can work around your schedule."

"We could?"

"Sure. It would beat slinging hamburgers."

Jeremy agreed. His brother, Tom, had spent many summers working in fast-food restaurants, but had counseled the younger Jeremy, "You've got a great brain, kid. Use it for something besides burger duty."

"I'll think about it."

His father nodded, then turned to the pile of work on his desk. "Much as I hate to cut you off . . ."

"No problem." Jeremy shot to his feet. "I'm tired anyway." In truth, he was wide awake. This was the best conversation he'd had with his father in months. For once they hadn't argued with each other. At the door, Jeremy paused. One other topic had been weighing on his mind. He decided to broach it, even if it spoiled the tenuous bond he and his father had just created. "Can I ask you something?"

"Sure."

"What do you think about people donating their organs?"

"It's a good idea. I mean, if a person's brain-dead, there's no reason for perfectly good organs to go into the ground when they could help somebody live. I see that very clearly now, especially in light of what's happening to Jessica."

Serious, Jeremy nodded and took a deep breath. "When Tom and I had the accident, were you and Mom asked to donate his organs?"

The air in the room grew perfectly still, and for a moment Jeremy regretted opening up the wound of his brother's untimely death. But his father only shrugged. "If we'd been asked, we might have. But there was so much damage to his body, I guess there was no need to ask."

Jeremy felt coldness creep over him. He had been removed by ambulance from the scene of the accident and hadn't seen his brother in the emergency room where they'd both been taken. And at the funeral, Tom had looked normal in the casket. It hadn't occurred to him that Tom might have suffered massive damage. *A tribute to the mortician's art,* he thought grimly. "I miss Tom," Jeremy said quietly.

"We all miss him," his father added. "But life goes on."

Jeremy turned and headed for his room.

The idea had been formulating in Jeremy's mind for a week before he decided to take action. On a Monday afternoon during the final week of school, he called Dr. Witherspoon's office at the medical complex where he practiced and made an appointment. Luckily the doctor had an opening, which Jeremy took as a good omen.

He made his way through the maze of hallways and elevators, let the doctor's nurse park him in a cubicle and was sitting on the examination table waiting when Dr. Witherspoon came into the room.

The doctor's eyes narrowed. "Haven't we met somewhere before?" He glanced at the chart with the information sheet Jeremy had filled out.

"I'm Jessica McMillan's friend."

The doctor broke into a smile. "Of course. I'm sorry I didn't recognize you at first. I didn't know you were in need of a nephrologist too."

"I'm not. I want to talk to you about Jessica."

"Doctors can't discuss their patients' cases. The information is privileged."

"I know, but I was hoping you could answer some questions I have about kidney transplants."

Dr. Witherspoon pulled up a chair. "Kidney transplantation is one of the most successful organ transplants we do. And best of all, a person can get along just fine with only one working kidney. That's what makes kidney donation so attractive between relatives. The patient gets a kidney, the donor continues to live a full, active life. Everybody wins."

"But what if you don't have a good match? How successful is it then?"

"With new antirejection drugs, over eighty percent of nonrelated donor kidneys are still functioning a year later."

Jeremy's heart began to race, and his thoughts surged with renewed hope. "Those are good odds."

"Yes." Dr. Witherspoon tipped his head and regarded Jeremy with curiosity. "I assume you have a reason for all this interest in kidney transplants."

Jeremy looked the doctor square in the eye and announced, "Dr. Witherspoon, I want to donate one of my kidneys to Jessica."

Chapter
7

"That's very admirable," Dr. Witherspoon said. His tone was noncommittal, but Jeremy did not miss the keen interest in the doctor's eyes.

"I know what you're thinking," Jeremy continued quickly. "You're thinking that I'm a nutty kid with a dumb crush on a girl and that I don't know what I'm saying. But that's not true. I know *exactly* what I'm saying. And yes, I like Jessica a lot, and how I feel about her is important, but it's more than that. I've seen Jessica change over the past months. I've seen how tough her life is. I know she's got problems with dialysis. What am I supposed to do?

I can't stand by and watch her die a little bit each day. I love her too much for that."

Dr. Witherspoon regarded Jeremy steadily during his impassioned speech and then answered calmly, "A doctor's first responsibility is to his patient. Frankly, there's nothing I'd like better than to take you up on your offer. We do numerous transplants at this hospital. In fact, we're one of the largest and best-staffed transplant centers in the country. Which is also a disadvantage because the waiting list is longer, currently up to eighteen months for a cadaver kidney. Therefore, live donors cut months, even years off the waiting process. But you're not a relative."

"That's true, but don't I have any say in who gets my kidney if I want to give it away?"

"Absolutely. The Uniform Anatomical Gift Act states that a person *can* designate an organ recipient. That's the law."

"Then if I want to donate a kidney and Jessica needs one and if antirejection drugs can help even if we're not perfectly compatible, then what's the problem?"

Dr. Witherspoon shifted in his chair. "Aside from blood-type testing—"

"I'm type O, like Jessie," Jeremy interrupted. He'd learned his blood type at the time of the accident. Although he had not been seriously injured, the hospital had typed and cross-matched his blood type as a precautionary measure.

"There's also HLA and MLC typing. These tests let us know if white blood cells will react against each other and whether or not antigens match. Since you're not a relative, it's highly unlikely your antigens will match."

"But you said that antigens don't always match and that you still do the transplant."

"Yes, using live, nonrelated donors is still controversial, but it's done. But back to you. You'd have to go through a battery of testing. First, we have to consider your general overall health."

"It's excellent."

"And there'll be psychological testing by a psychiatrist and a social worker."

"Why? It's *my* kidney!"

"They'll want to be certain you're emotionally stable and under no undo pressure. You're talking about giving away a part of your body, Jeremy. That's a big decision. Especially in your case because Jessica's not family."

Jeremy felt frustration building. He hadn't expected the doctor to try and talk him out of it. But he could see that Dr. Witherspoon was interested in finding an organ for Jessica; that gave him incentive to say, "I'll go through any testing you want. I'm sure I want to do this for Jessica."

Dr. Witherspoon contemplated Jeremy thoughtfully. The air in the examination room felt close and thick. Overhead, a fluorescent bulb hummed and flickered.

"This testing isn't inexpensive."

"I'm covered under medical insurance."

"Companies don't always pay unless the donors are related."

That surprised Jeremy. "There's no room for random acts of kindness?" The doctor smiled, and Jeremy waved aside the problem. "I'll worry about the money part later."

"There's one other problem." The doctor steepled his fingers and peered earnestly into Jeremy's eyes.

"What's that?"

"How old are you?"

"Sixteen. And a half." Jeremy felt his determination waver. "So what?"

"Legal age for medical-consent treatment is eighteen. That means you'd have to get a signed consent form from your parents before we can take your kidney. Or for that matter, do any testing on you."

Jeremy felt as if he'd been blindsided. He should have thought of that himself.

"Do you think they'll give their consent?" the doctor asked.

"Probably," Jeremy lied. "I mean they might not be for it at first, but if you'd talk to them—would you talk to them for me once I break the news?"

"Certainly." Dr. Witherspoon grinned. "It's not every day somebody walks into my office wanting to donate a kidney for a patient who needs one very much. No matter what comes of this, your gesture is admirable."

"I'm not doing it to be admirable," Jeremy said. "I'm doing it because I want to. Because I love Jessica and I want to do everything possible to help save her."

"Well, talk to your parents and get back to me." The doctor's beeper went off. "I've got patients to look after."

"No problem."

Dr. Witherspoon patted Jeremy's shoulder. "I'm in your corner. I'd like to see this work out, and I'll do everything I can to speed up the technical end of the process, if your parents give their consent."

Jeremy left the hospital feeling buoyed and energized. He had made it over the first hurdle. The doctor had actually listened to him, understood him and treated him as if he were a sane, rational person with a desire to help someone in need. Someone he loved.

Jeremy got in his car and started the engine. "One down, two to go," he muttered. Jessica and her family were the next people he had to convince. He'd save his parents for last. And once they heard from Dr. Witherspoon, how could they say no to his heartfelt request? How could they possibly deny Jessica this second chance at life?

"Happy Birthday, Jessie!"

Jessica blew out the eighteen candles on the

cake her mother set in front of her, and smiled at the three people who meant the most to her in all the world—her parents and Jeremy. How different this birthday was from the one the year before. Before her kidneys had failed. "The cake's beautiful, Mom."

She knew her mother had slaved for hours to create a cake that could be incorporated into her diet. She couldn't have much of it, and truthfully she wasn't even hungry, but she was determined to let her mother know how much she appreciated her effort. Especially now that Dr. Witherspoon had told them that neither parent could donate a kidney to her. They'd felt so awful about it.

"You should start a bakery, Ruth," her father said. "The recipes you come up with are sensational."

Her mother sent him a smile. "When this is over, I'll never *think* about cooking again. We'll eat every meal out after Jessie's better."

Jessica knew her mother had high hopes that the doctors would find her a donor kidney. Jessica was less optimistic.

"Open your presents," Jeremy said eagerly.

He'd been acting peculiar all day. Sort of antsy, as if he were a time bomb waiting to explode.

Jessica longed to really join the party. She wanted so much to please all of them. But she felt awful. Her dialysis the day before hadn't gone well. Her fistula had begun to clot, and now she was on blood-thinning medication and antibiotics. Her arm was sore. And already edema, swelling, had started in her ankles and feet. "Who's first?" she asked.

"Mine last," Jeremy said, snatching away the small box.

"Try ours." Her father handed her a narrow box wrapped with pink paper and a purple ribbon.

She tore open the paper and eased the top off the box. A glittering gold charm bracelet lay on a bed of white cotton. She caught her breath. "It's gorgeous!"

"Do you like it?" her mother asked. "We've already chosen a charm and thought we could add one for every special occasion."

A solid gold "18" dangled from the delicate chain of double links.

"It's perfect. You know I've always wanted one. Thanks so much."

"When you graduate, you'll get another charm." The ceremony was scheduled for Friday night in the civic auditorium. Jessica had her robe and mortarboard and at the ceremony would receive her diploma and tassel. *If* she felt up to walking across the stage.

"Don!" her mother admonished. "You weren't supposed to tell her. It was a surprise."

Her father blinked sheepishly. "Oops."

Jessica giggled. "I'll act surprised when I open it. Promise." She turned to Jeremy. "Well, are you going to let me have my present?"

He held out the box.

"It sure is small," she said teasingly.

"Big surprises come in small packages."

She unwrapped it and discovered another charm. This one was a bright gold kidney bean. "This is unusual."

He grinned. "It's not what it *is,* it's what it represents that's important."

"A bean? You think I'm full of beans?" She was having fun teasing him, watching his cheeks flush red.

"No. It's a kidney." He took a deep breath. "*My* kidney. I've already talked to Dr. Witherspoon about donating one of my kidneys to you."

For a stunned moment, no one spoke. Then everyone spoke at once.

Her mother started crying. "It's a miracle. An answer to prayer."

Her father gasped and began to bombard Jeremy with questions. "What? How? Are you *sure?*"

Jeremy held up his hands. "Wait a minute. I can't answer all of you at once." He grasped Jessica's hands and gazed lovingly into her eyes. "You first."

She was overcome with emotion; large tears pooled in her eyes. "You're the most wonderful person in the world, Jeremy." She swallowed against the lump of gratitude in her throat. "I appreciate your offer more than words can say. But I can't take your gift, Jeremy. I simply can't."

Chapter

8

Now it was Jeremy's turn to be astonished. "What are you saying, Jessie? Why won't you take my kidney?"

Her mother interjected, "Perhaps you shouldn't be so hasty, honey."

"Mom, please . . . I know what I'm doing."

"And I know what *I'm* doing," Jeremy said.

"Certainly there are plenty of questions to be asked—," her father started.

Jessica stood up, her fists clenched. "Mom, Dad, be quiet!" They looked crestfallen. More gently she asked, "Would you mind leaving me and Jeremy alone? I—I'd like to talk to him privately."

When her parents had gone, Jessica eased back into the dining room chair. "You should have told me what you wanted to do first. You shouldn't have sprung it on me in front of my parents."

"Okay, I'm sorry. But I thought you'd be happy. I *knew* they'd be."

So many emotions were tumbling through her that she was having trouble controlling them. Finally she said, "Your offer is mind-boggling. To even *think* about doing such a thing for somebody is awesome. Especially for someone who's not even related to you."

"I feel closer to you than to my own family. I—I love you, Jessie."

Tears welled again in her eyes. "And I love you. But . . . but in time, years from now, you may not feel that way. We may drift apart, find someone else—"

"Have you found another guy?" He looked alarmed.

"Don't be silly. There's no one else but you. And when would I have found this other guy? During dialysis treatments? Have you seen some of those patients? Most of them are older than God."

He shrugged sheepishly. Losing her was his greatest fear. "Then why talk about drifting apart?"

"Because it happens. You may not always feel the same way about me as you do now. What if we become bitter enemies?" He rolled his eyes at her suggestion. "The point is," she continued, ignoring his expression, "you'd have given me a kidney. You couldn't take it back."

"I don't give things away with the idea of taking them back."

"An organ isn't like the sweater you gave me for Christmas. Or this charm." She held up the gleaming gold jewelry. "It's *permanent*. It's gone from you forever."

Jeremy sensed her emotional distress, and he wanted to calm her, assure her that he understood the ramifications of his offer. He leaned forward and smoothed her hair, running his fingers through it. "Listen to me. You're right —I can't see the future. No one can. We may go our separate ways, although I'm not planning on it. But that's not why I'm doing this. I realize that giving you my kidney is far more complex than buying you charms and clothing.

"But think about something. Why is it all

right for a person to give someone he loves his feelings and emotions and not a tangible part of his body, when it could make such a difference in the quality of that person's life? Are my physical parts less valuable to you than my psychological ones? Less meaningful?"

"They're two different things altogether."

"Not to me. Stop treating me as if one part of me has more worth than another."

She wanted to stick to her original argument, that people just didn't go around giving organs away, but the look of sincerity on his face, the passion of his words were confusing her and making the action he was proposing to take seem more realistic. "But Jeremy, a *kidney*!" she cried in one last appeal to reason.

He pressed his fingertips against her lips. "Do you know how many people there are in the world who never get to do anything good, or kind, or noble? Who live all their lives and never make a difference? Who never contribute one single thing to make the world a better place? Or do something worthwhile for another human being?"

She couldn't deny it. Every day the newspapers and television reports were full of stories about people who did wicked and evil things. Who hurt and maimed, even killed. "I know there are bad people out there."

He shook his head. "That's not who I'm talking about. It's the rest of us—the ones who make up the majority." He sighed. "I want my life to count for something, Jessie. I want it to matter somehow that I was alive on planet Earth and that I left it a better place for having been born." His gaze dropped to his hands clasping hers on the white tablecloth. Shredded paper and limp ribbons lay beside their entwined fingers.

"I remember what my brother, Tom, always told me: 'Don't make a mess, kid, make a difference.' Giving you a kidney makes me feel good about myself and my life. It makes me feel worthwhile and useful."

"Jeremy, you have a whole lifetime to do something meaningful. You don't have to do it *now*."

"Why not? Now's the best time because no one knows how much time he has to live."

She knew he was thinking of his brother and the brutal end of Tom's young life. Jeremy's feelings about Tom were mixed up in his desire to donate his kidney to her, and she wasn't sure those feelings could ever be extricated. She wasn't sure it even mattered if they were. Jeremy's heart was in the right place. And his arguments were persuasive, so she knew he'd given his decision plenty of serious thought. She dared to hope that his plan just might work.

Another idea occurred to her. "What do your parents say about this?"

His face flushed. "I haven't exactly told them yet."

"Oh, Jeremy . . ." She kept seeing the hopeful expressions on her parents' faces turning to sadness, and she felt sorry for them. They wanted this for her. *She* wanted it for herself; but Jeremy's offer of a kidney was premature.

"But I plan to tell them tonight," he added hastily. "They may not be crazy about the idea at first, but I know they're really sorry about what's happened to you. And Dr. Witherspoon said he'd talk to them too."

She leaned forward until her forehead was touching his. "You know what I think? I think you're the kindest, most wonderful person in the whole world. No matter how this works out, I'll always be grateful for what you're trying to do for me."

"So you'll take the kidney?"

"You sound like Igor shopping around for body parts for Dr. Frankenstein. 'Excuse me,'" she mimicked, "'could you show me something nice in kidneys today? My boss is building this monster.'"

"Very funny." His mouth twitched into a grin. "This is serious. I want to do this for you. Please let me."

"If your parents approve, I'll do it," she told him. "You know how much I want to be off that machine." She kissed him lightly on the mouth. "Thank you, Jeremy. Thank you from the bottom of my heart."

"Are you out of your mind? Are you crazy? What makes you think your mother and I would even consider such a foolish idea?"

His father's explosive questions made Jeremy blanch. He hadn't been prepared for such a negative reaction. He looked at his mother but saw an expression of total disbelief on her face and knew he wasn't going to find support from her. "Stop treating me like I'm deranged," he told his parents. "I know what I'm doing."

His father leaped up from the sofa in the formal living room and stomped across the lush carpet. "Giving your kidney away is the stupidest notion that's ever entered your head. I know you like this girl, but this is *ridiculous*."

Jeremy also jumped to his feet. "It isn't stupid! Stop treating me like a baby."

"Then stop acting like one."

Jeremy was bewildered. He hadn't expected such a reaction. "I thought we were in agreement!" he shouted. "The other night when we discussed organ donation, you were all for it."

"Organ donation is a fine idea, but not when the person's still using the organ!"

"People do fine with one kidney. The body only needs one anyway."

"Then why did God see fit to give everybody two?"

"Maybe so we could share." Jeremy felt the elation of triumphing over his father. It was short-lived.

His father spun and glared at him with a look that would have melted steel. "Did you ever stop to think that your one kidney might one day be injured or become diseased? Then where would you be?"

"In the same place Jessie is—in need of a donor."

His father raked his hand through his hair. Jeremy could see him mentally shifting gears. He braced for another attack. "Your sentiments are noble, but misplaced. People don't give away their kidneys to perfect strangers."

Jeremy saw red. "Jessica isn't a stranger. You said you liked her. You told me that you and Mom both liked her." He looked to his mother again.

"We *do* like Jessica," his mother said hastily. "She's a wonderful girl. That's not the point."

"So what is the point?"

"She's not family, and she's not at death's door. Let her go on a waiting list like other patients. Sooner or later, a donor will be found."

Jeremy sputtered, "B-But she's not doing well on dialysis. And waiting for another live donor could take years." What was wrong with them? Why couldn't they understand? How could he explain it better?

All at once his father stopped pacing the floor and leveled a look of indignation straight at Jeremy. "I know what's going on here. She's using your attraction to her to make you *think* this is *your* idea. Jessica put you up to this, didn't she?"

Chapter
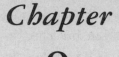

9

For a minute Jeremy was shocked speechless by his father's accusation. His hands shook, and his legs quivered with pent-up rage. He leaned heavily against the back of a chair, braced himself and took several deep breaths. "You have no right to say that. You have no right to *think* it. Jessica would never do such a thing. This was my idea and mine alone. When I told her about it, she told me no."

"At least *someone* is being sensible in this situation." His father must have sensed the depth of Jeremy's outrage, because his voice sounded less accusatory.

"But her parents were beside themselves with gratitude," Jeremy added.

"Her parents? You discussed this with her parents before you broached it with us?" His father's voice had grown hostile again. "Where do you get off—"

"Stop it!" His mother had risen unsteadily to her feet, her eyes brimming with tears. "I can't stand this! Do you hear me? I won't listen to the two of you tear each other apart. I won't!"

Frank Travino bounded across the room and pulled his wife into his arms. He glared at Jeremy. "Now see how you've upset your mother."

She jerked away from him. "You're both upsetting me. You can't fight like this. I can't take it."

"I'm sorry, Mom," Jeremy mumbled, feeling contrite. "I—I didn't mean to upset you. It's just that Jessica . . ." his voice trailed off.

His mother asked, "Don't you think I understand what her parents are going through? I know what it's like to stand by and watch your child die."

Jeremy winced. *Of course she knew.* Tom had died in the emergency room while his parents held his hands.

"This discussion is over," his father said tersely.

"Hear him out, Frank." His mother's command surprised both Jeremy and his father. She sat down on the couch, looking straight at Jeremy. "Tell us what you want to do."

Warily Jeremy stepped from behind the chair he was using for support, came to his mother and crouched down in front of her. "Thank you for listening to me," he said. Then he told them all he knew about organ transplantation. "Jessica's doctor, Dr. Witherspoon, can answer any questions you have," he said in conclusion. "We can go in together and talk to him if you want. He'd be in charge of the surgery, and he wants what's best for both Jessica and me."

"There are risks in surgery." His father renewed his objections. "You wouldn't be his primary concern. A doctor always puts his patient's interests first—just the way an attorney always puts his client's interests first."

"Frank, please," Jeremy's mother said, cutting off the counterargument already springing to Jeremy's lips. She looked into Jeremy's eyes. "Let me see if I've got this straight. In order for you to be a donor, you need to be some kind of match at the genetic level."

"Yes."

"And if you aren't a match, then this whole thing is dropped."

He didn't have the heart or the stamina at the moment to tell her that transplants could be done when there was no match. He figured it best to keep quiet at this point and be grateful for this bit of progress. "As I said, her doctor can answer any questions," he responded evasively.

"And," his mother continued, "they can determine if you're a match by simply doing blood work."

"Yes."

She looked up at her husband. "That doesn't seem so terrible, Frank. I mean a blood test seems harmless enough."

"I'm against this, Marilyn."

"They send a sample of my blood to a lab, Dad," Jeremy said eagerly. "At least let me take that step."

His mother was gazing up at his father with a look of resignation, and Jeremy knew by the expression on his father's face that he'd won this battle.

"I'll sign the papers for the blood test," Jeremy's father said shortly, his words clipped. "But that's all. One blood test."

Jeremy rose, suddenly exhausted. "Thank you." He was out the door when he heard his mother tell his father, "It'll be all right, Frank. We should allow him this much leeway. He loves the girl. I mean, he has to match her in some way, and what are the odds of that happening? I'd say a million to one."

"The odds aren't high enough for me," Jeremy heard his father say. "Not nearly high enough."

When Jessica's parents heard the news, they rushed over to Jeremy's house and spilled out their gratitude with handshakes and effusive speeches. Jeremy didn't miss his father's tight-lipped expression or his mother's polite but vacant stare.

"We'll pay for everything," Don McMillan said. "You don't have to worry about any of the costs."

"Is the test expensive?" Jeremy's mother asked.

"Between six and eight hundred dollars," Don said. "But who can put a price on Jessica's life?"

His parents didn't say anything negative. And when they met Dr. Witherspoon and signed the consent form, they asked no questions. It was as if they wanted only to get out of his office as quickly as possible.

"Are you certain there's nothing you want to know?" the doctor asked, placing the form in a manila folder.

"Nothing," Jeremy's father said. He cupped his hand around his wife's elbow. "It's understood that our consent is only for the antigen test."

"It's understood," Dr. Witherspoon said, "but as long as we're taking this first step, why not let me go ahead with the other testing? We'll check him into the hospital for a couple of days and get a complete picture of his eligibility as a donor."

"We'd rather not."

Jeremy watched the doctor's face and realized that Dr. Witherspoon knew exactly what he was up against. "The antigen test alone might not knock him out of contention," he told them. "However, the other testing may. We don't want to get Jessica's hopes up prematurely. Therefore, if you'd allow Jeremy to do the full battery of tests, it would give me the total picture as to his suitability as a donor."

Jeremy suppressed a smile. Dr. Witherspoon was clever, and he knew how to get what he wanted from the most reluctant people.

"Frank, perhaps that's not such a bad idea," Jeremy's mother said. "The psychological tests may show that Jeremy is unfit."

Jeremy didn't think so, but he kept his thoughts to himself.

"I think it's a bad idea," Frank told his wife. "But I said I'd cooperate through this point. So if the full battery of tests will settle this matter once and for all, go ahead."

Jeremy watched them march out of the office; he had a sinking feeling in the pit of his stomach. If the tests were favorable, he knew, he'd only just begun to fight.

———

Jessica's emotions swung wildly between euphoria and fear. She was ecstatic about the prospect of getting a new kidney, but terrified too. When Jeremy was admitted to the hospital for three days of intensive testing, she stayed with him as much as possible. It wasn't easy watching a perfectly healthy person go through blood work, X rays, an electrocardiogram, a renal arteriogram, and probing questions from a psychologist, all for her sake.

"My father's getting a perverse pleasure out of this," Jeremy told her the evening before he was to be discharged. They were sitting in a waiting area because he couldn't stand being cooped up in his hospital room. "He thinks all this medical stuff—the needles and machines —will scare me off. But it won't."

She'd had dialysis that day, but already a headache was gathering behind her eyes and her skin was starting to itch. "I feel bad for you," she told him. "You're going through so much just for me."

"If it were my brother who needed a kidney, they'd let me donate mine to him."

"But it isn't your brother."

"Yeah. Tom's dead. So I can't do anything

for him. But if he were alive, believe me, he'd be one hundred percent behind this."

"Well, all this may be for nothing anyway."

Jeremy clasped her hand. "No way, Jessie. The tests will show that I'm a compatible donor. I'm going through with the surgery." He'd made up his mind to be a nonrelated donor one way or another. And he felt strongly that Dr. Witherspoon would take him in order to help Jessica.

"Not without your parents' permission."

"Why is it necessary to get their permission for everything? I hate being sixteen. I wish I were eighteen. Then I'd be emancipated. Then I wouldn't have to ask them for anything."

"They're just worried about you. They care about you."

"Big deal. *I* care about you." She started to cry, and he took her into his arms. "I didn't mean to upset you," he apologized.

"The whole thing's upsetting, Jeremy. I feel like I have no control over anything. I've been accepted to Georgetown for the fall semester, but I'm afraid to make any long-term plans."

"It'll work out, Jessie. I promise."

"I still can't figure out why this is happening to me. Have I been a bad person? Did I do something to make God mad at me?" She couldn't stop sobbing.

"It's just life, Jessie. Like Tom's accident. Bad things happen, and nice people get crushed. There aren't any answers. You just have to believe that whatever happens is under someone's control, for some kind of purpose. If you don't, you'll go nuts."

She pulled away, staring deeply into his golden brown eyes. What she saw was no immature sixteen-year-old, but an insightful, comforting friend. What she saw was love, so open and honest that it wrenched her heart. She leaned forward and kissed him. And knew without a shadow of a doubt that Jeremy Travino was going to pass at least the psychological portions of his testing with flying colors. The rest of the test results would be in the hands of God.

Chapter
10

"If I hadn't read the results of the antigen test with my own eyes, I wouldn't have believed it." Dr. Witherspoon's voice boomed with enthusiasm.

Standing in the doctor's office with Jessica and her parents, Jeremy couldn't stop grinning. "Are you saying I'll make a good donor?"

"An amazingly good donor."

Jeremy felt as if a weight had been lifted from him. His parents would have to reconsider his desire to donate his kidney to Jessica.

Jessica's parents were both teary-eyed. They kept hugging Jeremy and saying "Thank you," but he scarcely heard them. He had eyes only for Jessica. She was sitting in a large leather chair, staring up at him in absolute amazement. He dropped to his knees in front of her. "Are you happy?"

"Numb," she confessed. "I never dreamed . . . "

"I dreamed it for both of us," he said softly. Despite the others in the room, he felt as if they were sealed off in their own private space.

He thought Jessica looked frail. She'd been steadily losing weight despite her mother's efforts to feed her properly. Yet her hands and legs were puffy and swollen with water weight. Her once thick and shining hair looked dull. Dark circles ringed her eyes. He knew instinctively that his compatibility as a donor hadn't come a day too soon.

Her gaze bore into his. "I want to be happy about it more than anything. But it's so *big*, Jeremy. A new kidney. *Your* kidney. An operation. Recovery. Being free to eat the things I like again."

"I'll buy you the biggest plate of french fries in Virginia when you're well," he said. She didn't smile. "Hey," he said, "you're not going to back out on me in this deal, are you?"

"You still have to get your parents to agree," she said, hedging.

"I'll do it." He wished he felt as confident as he was pretending to be. "Once they see how important this is, they'll fall in line."

"But, Jeremy, *you're* the one who's important to them. Not me."

"Then they'll just have to realign their priorities, won't they?"

She smiled. "You're very stubborn."

Dr. Witherspoon came over and placed his hand on Jeremy's shoulder. "I've been thinking; how'd you like me to talk to your parents about this first?"

Jeremy rose to face the doctor. "You?"

"I'm a professional, and I'm not involved to the same emotional degree as you are. I might be able to persuade them."

Jessica's parents stepped up beside the doctor. "We understand their reluctance," her father said. "It's a hard decision for a parent to make."

Feeling irritated, Jeremy asked, "What's so hard? It's *my* body. I should have a say-so in what I do with it."

"One step at a time," Dr. Witherspoon said. "Let me talk to them, explain the procedure. It isn't without risks, Jeremy. Any time a person goes under anesthesia, there are risks."

"Such as?"

Dr. Witherspoon glanced down at Jessica. "We can discuss them later."

"I don't care about the risks; I want to donate my kidney to Jessie. My *compatible* kidney," Jeremy added for emphasis.

"I'll call your father this afternoon and arrange for them to come to my office as soon as possible."

"I'll come too," Jeremy said.

The doctor shook his head. "That might not be a good idea. Let me talk to them as calmly as possible in neutral territory. I'll see what kind of progress I can make on my own."

That afternoon Jeremy returned to his father's law office. He'd taken his father up on his offer to be a law clerk. Fortunately his father was in court, so Jeremy didn't have to talk to him. He was afraid he wouldn't be able to keep his mouth shut about the test results, and he wanted Dr. Witherspoon to handle revealing the information. Also, he didn't want another volatile confrontation. He hated to hurt his mother, but his father was being impossibly stubborn.

Later Jeremy grabbed a burger at a fast-food drive-through, drove to Jessica's and called his mother, saying he wouldn't be home for dinner.

She said, "Your father and I are seeing Dr. Witherspoon tomorrow morning."

"Oh? Well, let me know what he tells you," Jeremy said as casually as he could.

"Your father and I love you, Jeremy."

Caught off guard, Jeremy stammered, "I—I know, Mom."

"And we only want to do what's best for you. Even . . . even if you don't agree."

Her statement sounded ominous. "Everybody wants to do 'what's best,'" Jeremy answered. "That's the problem. Sooner or later, someone has to give in."

Once he'd hung up, he took Jessica out to the backyard. Twilight was falling, and the June night closed around them like a soft whisper. Night-blooming jasmine perfumed the air. Overhead a violet sky was deepening to shades of midnight blue, and stars flickered on like fireflies. At the far end of the yard, between two thick tree trunks, a porch swing swayed. He sat Jessica down and settled beside her.

She inhaled deeply. "I love the smell of summer, don't you?"

He was preoccupied and had to force his mind to change course. He was alone with Jessica in the light of a pale moon rising. He needed to forget their problems and concentrate on her. "I love the smell of your hair," he countered.

"I have an appointment to get it all cut off next week."

"But why? I like your hair long, and you always have too."

"Because it looks terrible." She fingered it. "Kidney failure is ruining it, so I'll chop it off and stop feeling bad about the way it's looking. It's ugly."

"No—"

"Jeremy, it's okay. It's only hair."

He could tell that cutting it would be difficult for her, but that she'd made up her mind to do so. "You can grow it long again after the transplant," he said.

"Right," she said listlessly. " 'After the transplant' is beginning to sound like some foreign planet, some faraway destination where I'll never arrive."

"It's going to happen, Jessica." He hated to hear the sad resignation in her voice.

"I worry about it, though." She nibbled on her bottom lip. "It's a big responsibility—taking someone's organ from them. What if my body rejects it? Then everyone loses. You're minus a kidney. And I'm back on dialysis."

"Is that what's bothering you? You're afraid you'll reject my kidney?"

"Yes." She picked at peeling paint on the arm of the swing. "Dr. Witherspoon sent in a psychologist to talk to me. Some people aren't good transplant candidates because they don't plan on taking extra-good care of themselves."

"What'd you tell her?"

"I told her taking care of myself wouldn't be a problem for me. She said my fears are natural, that all recipients are uneasy about receiving another person's organ."

"And there's medication to keep you from rejecting."

"The drugs aren't guarantees, Jeremy. Sometimes, despite all the best care, a person still rejects."

He could see how deeply she was troubled by the idea. "Are you upset because you'll have to return to dialysis, or because you feel it's necessary to keep my kidney safe and healthy?"

She was amazed at his ability to instantly grasp her deepest, innermost feelings. At the bottom of her fears was the one about being inadequate, about being handed a responsibility that she might fail to live up to by default. "I don't want to reject *your* kidney," she mumbled.

"You're not less of a person if you do, Jessie. It's not something to be ashamed of, like cheating on an exam or stealing from someone."

She sighed and leaned her head against his shoulder. "Aren't you scared about losing an organ?"

He didn't answer immediately, and Jessica listened to the sounds of the night as she waited. Insects hummed, and water from the garden pond gurgled. Jeremy said, "It's more like anxious than scared. With the surgery, I go to sleep and a few hours later wake up with a sore side and back. They tell me I'll recover fast." He paused, and she heard a dog barking far away. "Maybe it has something to do with Tom's accident. I walked away with hardly a scratch while he died. I saw the car later; it was crumpled up like a squashed soda can. No one could figure out how I didn't get hurt. I sure don't know either."

She recalled the many discussions they'd had when their friendship was developing about his brother's death. Over time, he'd expressed anger, guilt, depression. But now his voice was different, as if he'd come to some kind of peace with it.

She listened as he continued. "You told me that God had saved me for a purpose. I've come to believe that the purpose was to help save you. Don't worry, I haven't got a God complex. But doing this for you is what I want to do. It's what I *need* to do. In a way, it helps me make sense out of Tom's dying while I'm still alive."

She could think of nothing to tell him that

would fully express her gratitude. She slid forward, turned to embrace him, and kissed him longingly on the mouth.

Jeremy was working in the law library the next day at noon, gathering books and articles for one of the attorneys in his father's office, when a secretary stuck her head through the doorway. "You've got a call on line three, Jeremy."

He quickly picked up the receiver. It was Dr. Witherspoon. Jeremy's hands grew clammy and his mouth went dry. "How'd the meeting go with my folks?"

The doctor sighed heavily. "Not well. I couldn't persuade them, son. I'm sorry. Your father is adamant about your not sacrificing your kidney, and there's no way he's going to relent."

Chapter

11

Jeremy hung up the phone. His parents weren't going to let him be Jessica's donor. In spite of all his pleading, all the information from Dr. Witherspoon, all the testing for compatibility, all the expressions of gratitude from Jessica's parents, it wasn't going to happen. Too numb to react, Jeremy sat and stared at the floor. He told himself to call Jessica, but he wasn't up to talking to her. Not yet. He needed time to think.

A rap on the law library door roused him from his stupor. His father stood in the doorway, his face a guarded mask. "I dropped your mother at her office. I thought you and I could discuss our meeting with Dr. Witherspoon."

"I heard about the meeting," Jeremy said, ignoring his father's offer.

"Your mother and I did what we think is right. I know our decision isn't popular, but it's the one we felt was in your best—"

"I know," Jeremy interrupted. "In *my* best interests."

"I hope you can be civilized about this."

"Sure. My girlfriend's dying and you won't let me help her."

"That's not fair, Jeremy. Her doctor will look for another donor. She's in capable hands."

Jeremy gave him a cold stare.

"Your mom and I aren't the bad guys in this, Jeremy. We're genuinely sorry about Jessica and we're willing to support and help out in any other way but this."

"It's my body," Jeremy muttered stubbornly.

"But it's our decision. When you're eighteen, you can do whatever you want—although even then I'd counsel against your donating. But for now, you're our responsibility and we're going to protect you from making an irrevocable choice."

"In two years, when I'm eighteen, Jessica may not be alive."

"You don't know that. No one knows what tomorrow holds for them, son. You may have a child someday who needs a kidney and you'd be unable to help him. Then you'd regret this decision."

Jeremy shook his head in disgust. "That's a far-fetched possibility."

"Anything can happen," his father said. *"Anything."*

"You know what's weird?" Jeremy didn't wait for his father's response. "I know you and Mom write a big check to the Humane Society and the Wildlife Preservation League, even that Save the Whales group every year. You have mercy on helpless animals, but not on people. You won't do a thing to let me help Jessica, and she's more valuable than any animal."

His father raked his hand through his short hair and sighed. "Listen, I've got a client coming in fifteen minutes. I can't stand here and argue this out with you right now. If you want to discuss it at home tonight—"

"No," Jeremy said calmly. "I'm through talking."

His father looked surprised. "Well, if you change your mind . . ."

"I won't."

When his father had gone down the hall to his office, Jeremy sat fingering the stack of law books. So, the battle was over. He had lost. *No! Jessica had lost.* He picked up the phone and dialed her number.

"I'm not mad at anybody, Jeremy." Jessica's voice sounded soft and breathy. Dr. Witherspoon had already called and broken the news to her family. "I don't have long to talk because Mom's taking me to dialysis soon, but I understand how your parents feel. I don't hold their decision against them."

He did. "What about *your* parents?"

"Mom's pretty shaken up, but Dad's more philosophical about it. He seems more understanding. He keeps saying we'll find some other donor."

"Can I see you later?"

She hesitated. "Maybe it would be better if you didn't come around for a few days."

He felt sick at her suggestion. And afraid they'd never let him see her again. "Why?"

"Just until Mom calms down. She's . . . mixed up . . . and angry." He could tell it was difficult for Jessica to talk to him about this. "Give her a few days to get a better perspective on things. She'll come around. I know she will."

"Things like me?"

"Things like the unfairness of life."

"I love you, Jessie."

"I love you too. That won't change."

He didn't want to hang up. Didn't want to sever the connection. He wanted to hold her, kiss her. Quietly he said, "It's not over, Jessie."

"What do you mean?"

"I'm going to find a way to do what I want to do."

"But—"

"But nothing. I won't let my father stop me."

Jeremy spent the next week working and keeping to himself. At home he hardly spoke to his parents. He was aloof and impersonal, and went out of his way to avoid them—leaving the room when they entered, eating no meals with them and staying in his room as much as possible. They didn't pressure him, content to give him the latitude to nurse his hurt and anger.

The worst part of his self-imposed exile was not seeing Jessica. If she didn't answer the phone when he called, her mother hung up on him. In a way, he didn't blame Mrs. McMillan. Her daughter was acutely ill, and her best chance for recovery had been snatched away. He had gotten their hopes up and then failed to deliver on his promise.

It was only mid-July, but the remainder of the summer stretched before him like an unbroken chain of dreary days and endless nights. He knew he'd have to do something to turn things around, not only for himself, but for Jessica.

He began spending his lunch hour poring over law books, making notes as he waded through the legalese. Slowly he began to formulate a plan, and as it started to coalesce, he began once again to find hope for Jessica's impossible situation. But he needed help to carry out his plan. Serious help.

He called Jessica's father, catching him by surprise. Jeremy said, "I need a favor."

"What kind of favor?"

"I want you to help me get in to see a law professor at Georgetown. A *good* law professor."

Don McMillan set up an appointment for Jeremy with one of the top professors of law at Georgetown University. On the night of the meeting, Jeremy drove to the campus, parked in front of the law building and went into the lobby.

Don McMillan was waiting for him. Jeremy held out his hand. "Thank you, sir, for helping me."

Jessica's father smiled wanly. "Judson Parker is a good friend of mine. And an excellent professor of law. We haven't seen much of each other ever since Jessica got sick, but he was willing to meet with us when I called and asked. Besides, Jeremy, I hold no ill will toward you. Your heart was in the right place when you tried to give Jessica . . . well, you know."

"How is she?" Jeremy had sneaked in to see her that very afternoon at the dialysis center. He'd come before her mother was to pick her up and had sat beside Jessica's chair, holding her hand while the machine finished cleansing her blood. They hadn't talked much; Jessica was ill. But being near her had calmed and comforted him. And it had given him renewed resolve to face tonight's meeting.

"She's not well," Don McMillan said in answer to Jeremy's question. "Dr. Witherspoon tells us she's struggling with high blood pressure and water retention, despite the dialysis. He's changed her medications again. That's the third time in four months."

Jeremy was dismayed.

Her father patted him on the back. "It's not your fault, Jeremy. Don't put yourself under so much pressure."

Jeremy knew he was talking about his parents' refusal to sign the consent form for the transplant. "I know," he said. "Maybe after tonight, though, I'll be in a position to turn things around."

Don led him into a lecture hall with built-in chairs on risers that angled down to a flat floor with a table, a podium, and a blackboard along the back wall. Tonight three people were seated around the table. Don introduced Jeremy to Professor Parker, who in turn introduced them both to the younger man and woman beside him. "This is Fran Beckner and Jacob Steiner, two fourth-year students and two of my brightest and best."

Jeremy's nervousness was calmed by the friendly smiles of the dark-haired Fran and the frizzy-haired Jacob. "Jake," the man said. "I prefer that people call me Jake."

Professor Parker offered Jeremy a chair at the table opposite them. "Don says you work at your father's law firm, but you have some legal questions."

"Yes," Jeremy said, taking a seat. Jessica's father settled next to him.

"Isn't there anyone at his firm who could help you?"

"No one."

"Travino . . ." Fran turned the name over thoughtfully. "Is your father *the*—"

"Yes," Jeremy said, cutting her off. "He is."

The two students exchanged glances.

"How can we help you?" Professor Parker asked.

Jeremy took a deep breath. "I want to be free of my parents' legal hold on my life. I want you to help me declare my emancipation."

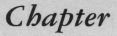

"Emancipation?" Professor Parker asked, sounding surprised. "Declaring independence from your parents is both serious and complicated."

"I know, but there's plenty of legal precedent for it." Jeremy reached into the portfolio he was carrying and removed a manila folder. He opened it, saying, "An eleven-year-old Florida boy filed to 'divorce' his biological parents and be adopted by his foster family. He won the case. Other kids have also been granted legal freedom from their biological families. I have some examples here." He handed Professor Parker several sheets of paper documenting his findings in legal books.

The professor skimmed Jeremy's notes. "These cases all involved abuse. Have your parents abused you?"

"No."

"Then on what grounds do you plan to petition the court?"

"Constitutional grounds."

Jake and Fran leaned forward. "Tell us."

"I believe that I should have the free will to decide what I want to do with my own body. And I believe that the Constitution of the United States grants me that privilege."

"Why do you want to take such a drastic action?" Jake asked.

Jeremy told them about Jessica, glancing at Don McMillan while he spoke. He kept his speech factual, trying not to color it with his emotions. "I passed every test the hospital gave me," he concluded. "Including mental competency. I was judged to be fully capable of making the decision to give away my kidney. I know exactly what I'm doing. And I know why I'm doing it. Without me, Jessica may die. I don't believe my parents should dictate to me what I do with my own body. But the only way I can donate my kidney and help save Jessica's

life is to remove myself from my parents' juris-
diction. I can't do that without your help."

Jessica's father touched Jeremy's arm. "Jeremy, are you certain?" His face looked pale.
"It's such a drastic step."

Fran drummed her fingers on the scarred ta-
bletop. "So you're asking the courts to decide
what constitutional right a minor has over his
own body? And when this right overrides pa-
rental authority?"

He was amazed at her quick evaluation of a
situation it had taken him weeks to define.
"Exactly," he answered.

She exchanged glances with Jake, and Jeremy could see that they were intrigued.

"Legal maneuvers cost money," Professor
Parker said. "Even if your attorneys work pro
bono—for free—there are court costs, filing
fees, things like that."

"Jessie's mother and I will pay all the costs,"
Don McMillan said quietly. "She's our daughter. And if Jeremy's willing to go to these
lengths to help her, we will aid him."

"You have a vested interest," Professor
Parker warned. "The courts may not like your
offering financial assistance."

"I'll take my chances," Jessica's father said.

"I have a trust fund set up by my grandfather for college," Jeremy said.

"There may be restrictions on it."

"I'll check." Jeremy started to hope that the law students might be willing to take up his cause.

Jake cleared his throat. "Your father's a powerful attorney with lots of connections. He won't take this lying down."

"I know." Jeremy held his breath.

Professor Parker stood up. "Let us take a few days to study this and talk it over. Your case is intriguing, but my law students may not be able to take it on. We'll call you."

"Not too long," Jeremy said. "Jessica's getting sicker every day." He shook hands with each of them, then headed for the door with Jessica's father. He still felt hopeful. They hadn't rejected him outright. And more encouragingly, the expressions on Jake's and Fran's faces had been downright predatory. He said to Don, "I think they'll take the case."

Don chuckled. "They certainly looked eager."

"Yeah," Jeremy said with a relieved grin. "Kind of like lions circling for the kill."

Don put his arm around Jeremy's shoulder. "Come to the house with me. I want you to break the news to Ruth and Jessica. We'll be with you, Jeremy. Every step of the way."

Jessica had very mixed feelings when she heard the news about what Jeremy was planning to do. Her mother had been ecstatic, but once Jessica was alone with Jeremy, she took him out to the swing and sat with him under the stars.

"Are you sure you know what you're doing?" she asked.

"How can you ask that? I *know* what I'm doing. It's the only way, Jessie, believe me."

"It's going to drive a wedge the size of a truck between you and your parents."

"They'll get over it. Once the operation is over and it's a success, they'll forgive me."

"But what if your father's right? What if something does go wrong?"

He placed his fingers across her lips. "Don't

say such things. Nothing's going to go wrong. That hospital transplants organs every day, and ours isn't even that complicated a procedure."

"But—"

"Then it will have been *my* choice," he said, interrupting her. "They won't ever have to blame themselves. Which in one way makes it far easier on them, if you know what I mean."

She understood, but she still felt scared. He was doing so much for her sake. She didn't deserve it. "How will I repay you?"

"By not rejecting me," he said, deadpan.

She giggled. "That's a sick joke."

"It made you laugh." He hugged her. "I've missed hearing you laugh."

"I've missed my former life—my LBD: Life Before Dialysis." She leaned back against his shoulder and stared up at the stars. "I missed the best half of my senior year. No prom. No senior skip day. No class prank. I hardly remember my graduation ceremony. It's all a blur. And this summer . . . well, my friends call and tell me all about shopping for college. About their vacations. Sara and Joanie got a place together down in Panama Beach, Florida, for a week. If I were well, I'd be going with them."

"You'll have it again," Jeremy said, hearing the longing in her voice. "Once the transplant is over and you adjust to the medications, you'll be healthy and happy."

"So if I have your kidney, does that mean we'll be related?"

"Kissin' kin," he joked. "I like that idea."

She pointed to the stars above. "I've wished on many a star. I've wished that I was normal again. Can I tell you a secret?"

"I can keep a secret."

"It's a serious one."

"I can keep a serious secret."

She paused; she was about to tell him something she'd never told anyone else. "I've thought long and hard about this, so I know what I'm saying. If I can't have a transplant, I don't want to go on living. You see, I don't think it's much of a life on dialysis. Maybe if things were better for me on the machine, I'd feel different. But I don't think so."

Jeremy nodded. "I don't blame you. I'd

feel the same way if it were happening to me."

"You would?"

He cradled her face in his hands. "That's why I'm trying so hard to give you my kidney. Neither of us would want to spend the rest of our lives married to a machine. No matter what, Jessie, I want you to know that I'm doing this for both of us."

She kissed him. "Win or lose," she whispered, "you're the best friend I'll ever have."

Two days later Jake Steiner called. Jeremy ducked into a vacant office and took the call. "Well, will you take my case?" he asked, getting right to the point.

"We'll take it."

Jubilant, Jeremy shouted, "Thanks!"

"It's going to be a dogfight when your father is served with the suit."

"I can fight. What's next?"

"Fran and I met for strategy planning, and we think the first course of action is to try and go through the juvenile courts."

"Why juvie court?"

"We can get our case heard more quickly. The docket isn't as full. And who knows? We just might get a sympathetic judge who'll grant us our request with no hassle."

Jeremy had never imagined it could be that simple. "How long?"

"First we serve the suit. Your father will have a week or so to respond to it. With a little luck, we can push for a quick hearing."

"How quick?"

"Thirty days. Maybe forty-five."

Dismayed, Jeremy said, "That's over a month! I don't know if Jessica can wait that long."

"We've checked with her doctor. He seems to think it will be all right."

"What did Dr. Witherspoon say about the suit?"

"He said that the hospital will support you in court if need be."

Jeremy's pulse raced. Having the hospital jump into the fray was more than he'd hoped for. And asking them was more than he would have thought about. It gave him confidence in his attorneys. They were young, but they knew how to fight. He began to think that he might have a chance of winning after all. "All right," he said. "Start the process."

"Keep us informed about what happens when the suit is served on your father."

"I won't have to," Jeremy said ruefully. "You'll be able to hear the explosion all over Washington."

Chapter

13

Jeremy thought he'd be prepared for his father's reaction when the suit was served. He wasn't. His father threw open the door of the mailroom where Jeremy was working. His face was livid, and for a moment Jeremy feared that his father might have a heart attack on the spot. Frank Travino railed at Jeremy, who only half listened to the tirade. Words and sentences such as "ingrate," "fool," "How dare you challenge my authority?" and "You'll never get away with this" peppered his speech.

Jeremy was dismayed but undaunted. His father ended his outburst with "I'll fight you

every step of the way. Don't think I won't."
Then he slammed the mailroom door with such
force that the doorjamb splintered.

Jeremy called Jake, who asked, "Want to reconsider?"

"No way."

"Your father knows the legal system, and
things are going to get worse before they get
better. You're going to be under a lot of pressure."

"I don't care. I'm not backing down."

But that night, at home, it was his mother's
tears that almost unraveled him. "Why are you
doing this?" she asked, weeping. "We love you,
Jeremy. You can't pit yourself against us like
this."

"It's not you, Mom," he said. "It's just that
this is *my* body and I should be able to do what
I want with it. What I want to do isn't illegal.
It isn't morally wrong. I should be able to decide."

"How has that girl eroded your loyalty to us
so deeply?"

He gritted his teeth so as not to yell at his
mother. "This is not Jessica's doing. It's mine."

"I know her family's helping you."

He felt his face flush. "Only with some of the finances. The whole thing is my idea. Please don't jump all over them."

Of course nothing was resolved, and the next day his father told him that he'd hired an attorney to handle his side of the case because he was too emotionally involved to plead the case himself. His father also fired Jeremy from his job. He couldn't take away his car because it had been a gift and Jeremy held the title, but without a job it would be difficult to pay for gas and insurance.

Jessica cried when she heard the news.

"It's only a job," Jeremy said, attempting to soothe her. "I can get another job. I can flip burgers with the best of them." He wanted to make her smile.

"It's not the job," she said, shaking her head. "It's what's happening to your family. I'm destroying your family."

Jeremy drove her to dialysis, all the while defending his actions and telling her not to worry. Her emotional condition was fragile, made more so by the buildup of toxins in her blood. When her treatment was over she was more subdued but still morose. Her mother invited Jeremy to dinner, and he accepted gratefully. He hadn't had a decent meal in days. The tension was so thick at his house that no one could eat.

When he arrived home that night, he was met by his mother's tears and his father's cold stare. "Your attorney called." His father fairly spat out the words.

Jeremy hurried upstairs and dialed Jake's number. Jake told him, "We have a court date. We're on the docket for the end of next month."

"That long?"

"Count your blessings. We're lucky to get on the docket so soon. The juvie court accepted our petition for extreme hardship and got us right in. Fran and I are preparing the case to present to the judge, but you might have to speak on your own behalf. Can you do it?"

"You bet. Will there be a jury?"

"Just the judge. There's no civil or criminal action being sought."

Jeremy felt a twinge of disappointment;

he'd imagined himself before a jury pleading his cause. "What if the judge knows my father?"

"It won't matter. We stand or fall on the viability of the suit."

Jeremy decided to ask about something else that had been weighing on his mind. "Jake, I think I should move out of my house until this is settled."

There was silence; then, "Things pretty tense over there?"

"Too tense. Plus it's tearing up my mother and I don't like seeing what this is doing to her. I can move into Jessica's. Her folks said it'll be all right with them."

"That's not such a good idea."

"Why not?"

"They have too much at stake and it won't look good for your case. The courts may interpret it as a form of subtle coercion on the McMillans' part."

"No one's coercing me," Jeremy snapped. "This is my idea."

"It doesn't matter. The courts might frown on it. Let's not take a chance."

"Then what should I do? I can't live here,

and my close friends are either out of town for the summer or not eager to get involved. At least their parents aren't." Jessica was his best friend; the two guys he knew best from school were his other choices, and neither of them could help him out.

Jake said, "I suppose you're right. You shouldn't be living at home through this process. Also, the situation might look more serious to a judge if you were living elsewhere. I mean, how serious could you be if you're still living under Daddy's roof?"

"So where should I go?" Anxiety began to gnaw at Jeremy. He'd never imagined he'd have to move out of the house he'd lived in all his life—at least not until he went away to college. He had a vision of himself sleeping in his car by the roadway.

"You could come stay with me," Jake said. "Just until this is over."

"With you?"

"I live alone near the college with a sleeper sofa you can take over. Just me and an old tomcat. Are you allergic?"

Jeremy heard the teasing tone in Jake's voice and realized that Jake must know how difficult this was for him. "I'll get another job," he said. "I'll help with the groceries."

"Darn right you will," Jake said with a laugh.

"When?"

"My guess is the sooner the better," Jake said. "How about this weekend?"

To his surprise, his parents didn't object to his moving. Obviously they too thought it best. "The furniture stays," his father said as Jeremy packed his clothes and some framed photographs. "And the computer."

"Don't worry, I won't take anything of *yours*," Jeremy tossed back sarcastically.

His mother remained dry-eyed, watching without speaking as he vacated the premises. She looked pale and bewildered, as if she couldn't comprehend how things had gotten to the point of her family's dissolving and falling apart in front of her.

He wanted to hug her good-bye and tell her he loved her, but it wasn't possible. They stood at the top of the stairs looking at each other as if a chasm had split the floor. Neither could bridge it. "Good-bye, Mom," he said.

She said nothing.

Jeremy drove out of Reston and into Georgetown, to a quaint area near the university where row after row of brownstone apartment buildings housed students and, occasionally, professors. Jake's place looked like all the others, reddish brown brick trimmed with colonial blue shutters. Jake told him where to park and helped him carry his stuff into the ground-level apartment.

"I really did clean the place up," Jake said, hanging some of Jeremy's clothes in the hall closet.

Jeremy set down a box he was carrying and glanced around the place he was to call home until—until when? He sighed. He didn't know how long he'd be in exile.

Jake's place had oak floors and a worn oriental carpet. Fancy electronic equipment lined one wall, and a sofa sat in the middle of the floor, facing the TV. "Your bed," Jake said, fluffing a sofa cushion.

"Thanks." A window air conditioner hummed, struggling against the gathering summer heat.

"Anything you see in the fridge is yours. Except the cat food." Jake grinned.

The cat sauntered into the room and stood still, staring at Jeremy and twitching his tail.

"This is Corpus Delicti, which is legal lingo for physical proof that a crime's been committed. And believe me, that cat's life is crime."

Jeremy knew Jake was trying to make him feel welcome, but at the moment he felt overwhelmed. He'd just moved out of his home. He was living with a stranger and his life seemed like a tangled mess. All because he'd tried to help someone he loved.

"I got a job at a car wash," he told Jake. "Hourly wage plus tips. I'll give you what I can every week."

"Hey, don't sweat it." Jake squeezed Jeremy's shoulder. "Fran's coming over tonight for a strategy session."

"Aren't you going to plead this on constitutional grounds?"

"Not in juvie court. Only federal courts rule on constitutional issues. But I'm hoping it doesn't go that route. I'm hoping we can get our way at this level."

Jeremy hoped so too. He wanted his life

back. Guiltily he remembered Jessica. She wanted her life back too, but without him she wouldn't get it.

Fran came over that night, and together she and Jake pored over the law books and scribbled notes. "Professor Parker said your father came to see him and tried to force him to bow out of this," she said.

"My dad did that?" Jeremy felt angry at his father all over again.

"I'm sure he's had us checked out too," Jake added.

Fran nodded. "Professor Parker told him that you were entitled to legal recourse just like anyone else." She chuckled. "Nobody backs Judson Parker down."

Jeremy was grateful that the professor could stand up to his father. He only hoped the judge who heard their case would too. He began to plan what he wanted to say to the judge, how he would convince him that he was an adult.

When the court date arrived two weeks later, he knew he was ready to face the judge. And his father.

Chapter
14

Juvenile court teemed with activity. Jeremy wore a suit and tie and felt like an absolute geek. Every kid sitting in the halls and court-rooms wore casual summer clothes, and they all appraised him with sneers. "Some of these kids are children," he said to Jake as they walked down the hall. Many didn't look to be more than twelve years old.

"Some of these children are seasoned felons," Jake countered.

"Don't let their youthful faces fool you," Fran added. "They all know that they won't be tried as adults so long as they're 'just kids,' and some have rap sheets as long as your arm."

At the end of the hall, they took an elevator

up. "We'll be heard in Judge Monsanto's chambers," Fran said.

Jeremy was relieved. At least they wouldn't be discussing their case in front of a busy courtroom full of strangers. "I'm looking for Jessica's parents," he said. "I thought they might be here."

"We told them not to show," Fran explained. "This is a closed hearing, so there's nothing they can do but wait outside. Plus, it's best if they keep a very low profile. We need the judge to be swayed to our side solely on the merits of the central issue: Why should your age be a factor in your desire to donate your kidney?"

They stepped into Judge Monsanto's reception area. Jeremy's father and his attorney were already waiting. Jeremy avoided their gazes. A woman came forward. "I'm the judge's secretary. He'll call you in momentarily. Would you like anything—coffee, a soda?"

They declined. Jeremy sat on the edge of a chair and stared at the floor, but from the corner of his eye he sized up the competition. Like his father, his father's lawyer looked polished and self-assured, wearing an impeccably tailored suit and custom-made leather shoes. His father had spared no expense in securing legal counsel. Next to the two of them Jake and Fran looked dowdy, resembling a ragtag army of dissidents with sticks facing generals who commanded a battalion of high-tech war machines. Jeremy shivered as a premonition shot through him. *We're going to lose!*

He was startled when the judge's secretary invited them into his chambers. In the judge's office were floor-to-ceiling bookcases, a large, heavy desk of dark wood and a conference table, and Judge Monsanto, a heavyset African American man with a bald head and black-rimmed glasses. In a deep, firm voice he said, "Please sit," and pointed to the table.

Each side sat opposite the other, and the judge took a seat at the head of the table. A pile of files lay in front of him. "I've reviewed your petitions carefully," he said, getting right to the point. He turned to Jeremy. "What you want to do is an amazing sacrifice, young man."

Jeremy was glad he was sitting because his knees felt shaky. "It's not really a sacrifice to me, sir." Jake had directed him to respond respectfully. Not that he wouldn't have anyway. That was the way he'd been raised.

"And I can certainly understand why your parents object. Goodness, I have trouble enough parting with a bad tooth in the dentist's chair, and you want to go through a complicated surgery to have your kidney removed."

Jeremy hadn't expected the judge to be so informal. He relaxed slightly.

"Still," the judge continued, "I've read the reports submitted by the hospital concerning your tests. You appear to be a prime donor candidate for this young woman. And your psychological evaluation was especially favorable."

"I tried to be honest," Jeremy offered hopefully.

The judge smiled kindly. "And your IQ is amazing. All in all, I'd say you're a remarkable kid with both feet on the ground." He shuffled through some papers. "I don't get many through my courts like you, Jeremy."

Jeremy nodded politely.

"Most of the sixteen-year-olds I get are pretty hardened. They know the system inside and out, and they know how to beat it. Tough kids." He shook his head.

Jeremy wondered if he'd missed some information along the way. The judge appeared to be rambling. Yet, he resisted the urge to hurry the man up.

"I want to ask you something." The judge looked straight at him. "I want you to answer honestly." He paused. "Have your parents ever mistreated you?"

Jeremy saw his father tense, but neither he nor his attorney spoke. "No, sir," Jeremy said.

"How would you say they've treated you?"

"They've treated me fine."

"Clothes, food . . . plenty of that kind of stuff?"

"Yes." Although things had been different around the house since Tom's death, his parents had never stopped attending to his needs.

"Discipline? You know, have they taught you right from wrong and made you toe the line when you disobeyed?"

"Yes, sir."

"But they never battered you or anything if you stepped out of line."

"No, sir."

"I wish all the kids who came before me could say that about their home life." He shrugged. "If that were the case, why, I'd be out of a job!" He flashed a toothy smile. "Except for the hard-core types. I mean, there are some kids who are born mean and no amount of good parenting can fix them."

Jeremy was thoroughly confused. He'd expected the judge to ask him about Jessica and his reasons for wanting to give her his kidney. Instead, he was going on and on about things that didn't make any sense. "I suppose," Jeremy said.

"But you've got good parents, isn't that right?"

"Yes."

The judge leaned forward. "You have a car?"

"Yes, but—"

The judge cut him off with a wave of his hand. "Lucky you. A lot of the boys I see in my court *steal* cars." He chuckled. "And since you're such a smart young man . . ." He flipped through some papers. "It says here you skipped a year in school and make excellent grades. Would you say your parents would send you to any college you wanted?"

"Probably. If I met the entrance requirements." Jeremy was starting to feel angry.

Why was the judge meandering so much? Why didn't he get to the real reason they were all there?

"So, Jeremy, let me see if I understand. What you're asking is that you be emancipated, set free, from loving, caring parents who have nurtured you, taken care of you, housed, schooled and fed you with love and devotion all your life."

Jeremy felt color rising in his face. "That's not the point." He looked at Jake, who had opened his mouth to speak.

The judge stopped the young law student with a look. "I'm still talking." He turned back to Jeremy. "As far as I'm concerned, that *is* the point. According to the law, the criterion for granting emancipation is the *best* interests of the child."

"I'm not a child!" Jeremy exclaimed before he could stop himself.

The judge reared back and pointed at Jeremy. "You are in the eyes of Virginia law, son. You're a minor under your parents' domain, and I see no reason to alter that situation."

Angrily Jeremy stood. "That's not fair! You're not thinking about Jessica."

The judge ignored his outburst. "I've read the hospital reports about the young woman in question. I've talked to her doctor. She too is under excellent care. And her situation is not critical."

"But—"

"I will not grant your petition," the judge said, closing his file folder.

Jeremy spun, furious and not sure what he might say to the judge. He heard the others standing up behind him, and as he moved to the door he saw his father coming toward him. *If he thinks we're going to kiss and make up, he's crazy!* Jeremy thought. He jerked open the door and yelled, "I'll see you back at your place, Jake."

He stormed out of the reception area, past the startled secretary, and ran down the hall toward the courthouse entrance. He had lost! He'd never even had a chance to say all the things he'd wanted to say. He had lost the most important battle of his life. Of Jessica's life.

And his father had won. He had won without saying a single word.

———

"We'll appeal," Jake said the minute he and Fran walked into the apartment.

"We'll file a de novo appeal, which means it's as if the decision never happened," Fran added. "And this time we'll go through a higher court."

"Don't you get it?" Jeremy stopped his restless pacing. His stomach was in knots and his skin felt as if it were on fire. "Jessica hasn't got any time!"

"Jeremy, this isn't the end of the world." Jake tried to soothe him. The phone rang and he said to Fran, "Get that, would you?"

"It's probably my father," Jeremy muttered as Fran crossed the room. "Probably calling to rub it in and tell me all's forgiven and I can come home now."

"I know you're upset," Jake said, "but this isn't over. It's a setback, but we still have several options. I'll file a writ of habeas corpus. And this time we'll go through the federal courts. We should have gone to the federal level from the start the way you wanted. Your idea to try this on constitutional grounds was a brilliant—"

He was interrupted by Fran, who had hung

up the phone and moved to Jeremy's side. "The stakes have gotten a whole lot higher," she said, touching Jeremy's arm. "That was Jessica's father. She's just been rushed to the hospital."

Chapter

15

Jessica stared up at the ceiling of her hospital room from her bed, the covers balled in her fists, tears of pain and frustration running down her cheeks. *Why is this happening?* she screamed silently. Why couldn't the terrible nightmare of kidney failure be over?

From down the hall she heard the rattle of supper trays arriving. When her meal tray was brought to her, it would be filled with "allowable" food, not the things she craved. Sometimes she dreamed about hot french fries, saturated with grease and salt, still sizzling. She swiped at her tears.

"Jessica! Are you all right?" Jeremy bolted through the doorway, skidded to a halt beside her bed and gently took her in his arms. "I got here as soon as I could. What's going on?"

She dissolved into tears again, pressing her face into his suit coat to muffle her sobs. "The fistula in my arm's collapsed," she managed to say. "Now they have to try and create another one in my leg. I go into surgery tomorrow."

"I'm sorry," he said over and over, stroking her hair until her tears slowed and her body stopped trembling.

"I'm so tired of this, Jeremy. Nothing's going right for me."

He looked away.

She settled back onto the bed, reached for a tissue and blew her nose. "I guess I've ruined your suit." She dabbed at the wet stains on the shoulder and lapel with another tissue.

"I don't care about the suit," he said, taking the tissue from her hand and dropping it into the wastebasket. "Tell me about you. And about what Dr. Witherspoon is doing for you."

"I'll have to return to an external shunt until my new fistula gets strong enough to do its job." The first fistula that had failed had also taken a month to become serviceable. The cannula, or tube, of the external shunt that Jessica would use in the interim ran down the outside of her arm, making it far harder to hide than the internal fistula. "It's ugly, Jeremy. I hate it. And it'll probably get infected. Why not? Nothing else's gone right for me."

"But at least it'll be easier to get the needles from the dialyzer into you," he reminded her. "You won't have to get stuck every time."

She wasn't consoled. "I feel like I'm starting back at square one, Jeremy. Like I'm in a terrible game that makes me start over just when I think I'm on top of it."

"But even with the external shunt, you can go home after the surgery and go back to your regular dialysis schedule."

The concern she saw in his dark eyes touched her deeply, and she regretted having unloaded on him. "Oh my gosh, Jeremy. The hearing! The hearing was today in juvenile court. You went through the whole thing for me, and I was having such a pity party that I didn't even ask about it. How did it go?"

"You weren't having a pity party," he countered. "You're in the hospital. I think you're entitled to be upset. The second I heard, I rushed right over. Where're your parents?"

"I made them go to the cafeteria. Mom's so uptight she might have to check into a room herself." Jessica sniffed and offered a wan smile. "I worry about them both, you know." She took Jeremy's hand. "Tell me what happened today."

He looked down at their joined hands, and she realized that because he was avoiding the subject, the hearing must not have gone well. She braced for his news.

"My father and his attorney ate us for lunch," Jeremy confessed quietly.

She felt another wave of depression. "So we lost."

He took her face between his palms and said fiercely, "We may have lost the battle, but not the war. We're not giving up, Jessie."

"Tell me all about it."

He did. "The judge wouldn't even let me speak except to answer his dumb questions," he concluded. "He made me feel like I was some sort of spoiled, snotty-nosed kid who didn't know that I was well off. Geez, I know I've got good parents. That's not what this is about. It's about my parents allowing me to do what I want with my own body."

He looked disgusted, and she felt so dismal, so defeated that she could hardly stand to have him look at her. "What's the use of fighting?" she asked.

"Because I've got a good case. Jake and Fran both think I can win if we go before a federal judge."

"But the last case took a month to be heard."

He nodded. "And getting a hearing set before a federal judge can take longer, but we'll file for extreme hardship like we did before. Maybe this judge will be more understanding, more favorable."

She shook her head. "Your father will only appeal the decision if you win."

"If he does, we'll go to a higher court. We'll go all the way to the Supreme Court if we have to."

She wasn't encouraged. "Don't you see, Jeremy, this could drag on for years."

He didn't say anything, and she knew her assessment was correct.

"I may not have years," she told him quietly.

He pulled her against his chest. "Don't say

that, Jessie. Don't ever say that. We'll find a way through this."

She allowed him to reassure her without argument, but she didn't feel hopeful in the least. They were two kids up against a world of powerful and knowledgeable adults who were convinced that they knew what was best for all concerned. But she didn't want to let on to Jeremy how defeated she felt. He was trying so hard.

She pushed away and changed the subject. "Another thing's got me down too. All my friends are packing and buying stuff for their dorm rooms, getting ready to go off to college. I was supposed to start classes too, but now I don't think I can hack freshman orientation, new class work and dialysis."

"Yeah," he said glumly. "I was hoping you could start in September like all your friends. Maybe things will be better by second term. Lots of people start college in January, you know. There's no law that says you have to begin in September."

She didn't want to think about it. All her plans and dreams had been totally altered by her kidney failure, and it was too painful to remember them. "What about you? You're going to be a senior and your senior year is supposed to be fun. Mine was . . . until this happened."

He shook his head. "I'm not going back to high school. I can't live with Jake and commute to Reston every day. And I don't want to start over in another school district."

"You can't drop out of school!" she cried, horrified.

"I can test out. I'm smart, remember?" He gave a rueful smile. "At least that's what the judge told me."

"But it's your senior year!"

"The only reason I hung around in high school at all was because of you, Jessie. I looked forward to that English class with you. Just seeing you in the halls and the cafeteria perked up my day. Don't you see? *You* were the only thing that kept me in high school in the first place."

"What about the prom and graduation ceremony?"

"You didn't go to your prom."

"And you know why."

He brushed it off. "And as for graduating, I

can get into college without a high-school diploma if I test high enough. In fact, I plan to graduate from college *without* a high-school diploma." He grinned. "Others have done it, so can I."

She didn't like it. She felt responsible for the course his life was taking. If it weren't for her, he'd be living at home, at peace with his parents, planning to return to high school. He wouldn't be embroiled in a tedious legal dispute. "If it weren't for me—," she began.

He silenced her with a quick kiss. "If it weren't for you, I'd never have known what it feels like to love somebody the way I love you."

She knew his words were supposed to make her feel better, but they didn't. They made her feel guilty, and responsible for his choices. She wanted to release him from the debt he seemed to think he owed her. She told herself that once she returned home, she'd think of a way to set Jeremy free.

It was late when Jeremy returned to Jake's. The TV was on, and Jake was watching a news program. "You're on my bed," Jeremy said. "And I'm whipped."

Jake asked, "How's Jessica?"

Jeremy told him, including the depression he sensed she was experiencing. He dropped onto the sofa and rubbed his neck. "Anyway, I gave her a pep talk, but I'm not sure it registered."

Jake pushed the Mute button on the TV remote. "I'm sorry about the way things went today. Fran and I feel responsible for the defeat."

"It was a calculated risk. We all knew that. My father's got legal experience, and worse, he's got time on his side."

Jake looked at him, and Jeremy could tell he was holding something back. "What's up?"

Jake grinned. "So much for a poker face, huh? Guess I'll have to do better if I ever get to go in front of a jury."

Jeremy watched him fidget, and a sudden stab of fear made him blurt, "You're not planning on quitting on me, are you?"

"No, nothing like that. But something has come up. Your father called earlier this evening. He wants a meeting with you, Jeremy. He wants to talk to you face-to-face."

Chapter

16

"He wants a meeting—why? To gloat?" Jeremy headed into the kitchen, and Jake followed him.

"I don't think his motive is gloating. I think he just wants to talk to you."

"We've already said all there is to say." Jeremy jerked open the refrigerator door and rummaged through the shelves. He wasn't hungry, only restless and agitated.

"He asked me if we were going to appeal today's decision and I told him we were."

"So, did he bite your head off because you're helping me?"

"No. But he and I both know what we're up against in the system."

Jeremy slammed the refrigerator door. "Don't tell me our lousy odds, Jake. I hate hearing the odds."

Jake caught his arm. "Jeremy, I think you should meet with your father."

"I don't."

"Listen to me. I'm your attorney and I'm advising you to sit down and talk to him again. Perhaps we can settle this case without going to court."

Jeremy boosted himself up onto the countertop and stared glumly at the floor. "He'll only drop his case if I give up my suit. And I'll only give up if he lets me do what I want. I'm telling you, Jake, he's not going to quit. You don't know my father. For him, winning is everything."

"One of the first rules of practicing law is to avoid litigation whenever possible," Jake said earnestly. "As your attorney, I'm advising you to see your father. I can arrange for the meeting in neutral territory—one of the conference rooms at Georgetown, for instance. I'll hang around in the hall during the meeting. And if the two of you come to blows, I'll run inside and throw myself between you." He grinned, and Jeremy returned a halfhearted smile.

"All right. But not until after Jessica's surgery. And not until she's out of the hospital and back into her everyday routine. I want to be there for her. She comes first."

Her surgery went well, and in a couple of days Jessica returned home. This time the external shunt was on her leg, capped off but accessible to the nurses in the dialysis unit. Dr. Witherspoon told her, "You're doing fine," but he prescribed a mild mood-elevating medication to combat her depression.

At home, Jessica lined up on her dresser the bottles of medications she took daily. The bottles stood like little brown soldiers awaiting their missions, from phosphate and potassium binders to calcium and iron supplements, plus numerous others to keep her body up and running. She remembered the days when her dresser had held bottles of perfume and makeup. Now those had been relegated to a drawer.

The phone rang and she answered it. Jeremy said, "How about a movie tonight?"

"Yes," she told him. She wanted to escape from her dreary everyday life, if only for a few hours. "I need to go out and do something normal."

The theater was packed, and the smell of buttered popcorn made her mouth water. Her snack consisted of a measured amount of jelly beans and a diet soda. Jeremy stuck to snacking on hard candy and soda—in deference to her, she figured.

Afterward they went to a nearby coffee shop and ordered specialty coffees. "I'd kill for some french fries," she said with a sigh. "I thought I was going to have to ask the guy sitting next to me with his bucket of popcorn to move. The smell was making me crazy."

"Once you get your transplant, you can pig out on french fries and popcorn too."

"Sounds heavenly to me." They rarely discussed the actual transplant anymore because it was too depressing.

"I've agreed to see my father this Friday," Jeremy said quietly.

"You have? But that's good. You shouldn't be estranged from him."

"I'm doing it for two reasons: Jake wants me to, and I know you do too."

She stirred her coffee, watching Jeremy's face. "What do you think he wants?"

"Probably wants to offer me a deal, his kidney for mine," he said sardonically.

She giggled. "Maybe he just wants to kiss and make up."

"He knows how he can make up with me."

She leaned back and propped her feet up on another chair. Sitting for so long in the movie had caused her legs and feet to swell. Her shoes felt tight, but she was afraid to take them off; she might not be able to get them back on. "Did I tell you that I persuaded my mom to go back to her Head Start job? She was planning on not returning this school year, but I told her I wanted her to work. She gets too preoccupied with my kidney problem and drives me nuts with her hovering. I have to take over someday." She paused. "I'm thinking of getting my own apartment, Jeremy."

He sat up straight. "When?"

"As soon as I can. I need to be out on my own."

"Then why not go to college? You can live in the dorm if you don't want to live at home."

"I'm not ready yet. Maybe in January, like you suggested. But right now I want to learn how to cope on my own. This is *my* kidney problem. Not my parents'. Not yours."

He looked hurt. "I didn't mean to make you feel as if I was taking it over."

"I know you care. But things should never have gone this far. You at war with your family. You living with a stranger. You dropping out of high school. Things have simply gotten out of hand, and I feel like it's my fault."

He opened his mouth to protest.

"Let me finish," she told him. "I've been wanting to say this for weeks. I think you should drop your emancipation suit, Jeremy."

"I don't want to."

"Why not?"

"Because you need my kidney."

She shook her head. "I *need* a transplant. I would *like* to have your kidney."

"It makes no sense to me that you shouldn't have my kidney."

"Let's not argue. All I'm trying to say is that

I need to handle my own problems. If your father offers you an olive branch on Friday, take it."

His lips pressed into a thin line of stubbornness. She reached out and took his hand. "Make peace with your father. Don't turn this suit into a contest of wills. Because if you do, no matter how it turns out, no matter what a judge rules, both you and your father will be losers."

On Friday Jeremy dressed with care. He didn't want to go to the meeting looking or feeling like a kid. When he walked into the living room of the apartment, Jake looked up from his seat on the sofa. "Not bad, Jeremy. Is that my silk dress shirt?"

Jeremy grinned sheepishly. "And your silk tie. Your stuff goes pretty good with my blue suit, don't you agree?"

Jake grinned back. "No contest. Don't get it messed up."

"Not to worry. I promised Jessica I'd try to bury the hatchet."

"Just don't bury it in your father."

Jeremy groaned at Jake's bad joke. It wasn't going to be easy to face his father, especially after their day in court two weeks before.

He had a stomach full of butterflies as he and Jake drove to the campus. Jeremy glanced at his watch and thought about Jessica. She'd be almost through with her dialysis treatment by now. In his mind's eye he saw the treatment center, the rows of recliners, the small dialysis machines, the many patients. He felt a pang of regret. More than anything, he'd wanted to change things for her, to free her from the machine and make her life better. All he'd succeeded in doing was to bring more tension into her life.

Jake interrupted his thoughts. "It's best to take your cue from your father. If he wants to be belligerent and antagonistic, get out of the room. I'll step in and tell him that our next stop is federal court. Fran is writing a new brief as we speak."

"Good. I still don't want to give up."

"Just don't go into the room with any preconceived ideas," Jake counseled. "Anything can happen, Jeremy. Anything."

Jessica left the dialysis unit feeling better than she had in weeks. It was early September, and she thought back to the previous Labor Day. Her parents had taken two rooms at an oceanfront hotel in Virginia Beach, and they'd had a wonderful time. Jeremy had driven down, and together they'd swum in the cool Atlantic water, walked the beach at night hand in hand, and danced at a small bistro that catered to the teen crowd.

She smiled at the memory. Even though she'd been experiencing some signs of kidney failure, she'd ignored them and had had one of the best times of her life. *Who knew?* she asked herself. What a difference a year made!

She slid behind the wheel of the car and turned on the air-conditioning to cool the steamy interior. This whole summer had slipped past, and Jessica had few good memories. Enviously she thought about her friends who'd gone to the beach in Florida. Maybe next summer, if she was still on dialysis, she could locate a dialysis center near the shore and take her treatments *and* spend time at the beach.

On a whim, she checked the car's glove compartment and found a map of Virginia. Eagerly she traced a line with her finger from Washington to Virginia Beach. It was expressway all the way. And according to the legend at the top of the map, it was only two hundred miles to Virginia Beach.

Suddenly she was seized with an intense longing to see the ocean, smell the salt air, walk barefoot in the rolling surf. She looked at the clock on the dashboard. It was just barely noon. She'd been going for dialysis early on Fridays during the summer in order to have a long weekend. So why not take advantage of it? If she left now, she could make it to the beach in three hours. She could visit the ocean, eat dinner on the pier, watch the moon rise and still be home before eleven.

Jessica felt a tingle of excitement. *Why not?* Her parents weren't scheduled to be home until six tonight. She could call them from the pier and tell them what she was doing. No way could she call before she left; they'd be adamant that she not make the trip. If she waited until later, there'd be nothing they could say except "Come home now!"

If only Jeremy could go with her . . . but

he was about to meet with his father. She grinned and, feeling like a child playing hooky, eased the car into traffic and drove toward the expressway and Virginia Beach. She headed toward the ocean and a few precious hours of freedom.

Chapter

17

"How are you, son?"

Jeremy stood awkwardly in the small conference room, looking at his father's lined face, unsure whether he should shake his hand. Frank Travino looked tired and thinner than he had when Jeremy had moved out.

"I'm doing fine," Jeremy answered, then crossed to the oval conference table and took a seat. "How's Mom?"

His father sat across from him. "Physically, she's fine, but emotionally . . ." His voice trailed off.

Jeremy gritted his teeth, not wanting to rise to the bait. "This has been hard on all of us emotionally," he said. "I never intended to hurt anybody—especially Mom."

"She—um—she wanted me to tell you that she misses you and to ask you to please come home."

"I don't think I can do that yet."

"I want you to come home too. We both miss you."

Jeremy knew the admission wasn't easy for his father, but he also knew he couldn't give in to emotional blackmail. "Jessica still needs my kidney," he said quietly.

"You lost in court."

"I lost in *one* court. There are others."

"Yes, your attorney told me you will appeal."

Jeremy nodded, not wanting to reveal any more information than necessary. He knew enough to let Jake handle any legal discussion of the case.

"You'll lose again," his father said matter-of-factly.

Jeremy felt his anger rising. "If I do, I'll try again."

"The process can take a long time."

He was telling Jeremy much the same thing Jessica had. But coming from her, it hadn't sounded so threatening.

"Is that what you're hoping? That the process will take so long that Jessica will die?"

"Of course not—"

"Or that her doctors will find another donor?" he added, interrupting his father.

"Would that bother you? Would it matter if she ended up with another person's kidney?"

"Why should it matter? Just so long as she's okay."

His father drummed his fingers on the table-top. "Because then you couldn't be the hero."

Shocked, Jeremy bolted to his feet. "Is that what you think I'm trying to be? A hero? Let me explain it to you one more time—in case you don't remember." He felt hot. "Jessica doesn't tolerate dialysis very well. She needs a transplant. No one in her family can be a donor. She's not a candidate for a cadaver kidney. I was willing to be a noncompatible donor, but wonder of wonders, the tests showed me to be a good match. Therefore, she has less of a chance of rejecting my kidney. Which means that she can return to a more normal life. Go to college. Get a job. Maybe even grow old.''

His father rose too. "Calm down. I didn't come here to fight with you. Can't you sit down and listen to what I came to say?''

Jeremy didn't want to calm down. He wanted to get out of the room and slam the door behind him. But he kept hearing Jessica's voice telling him to *make peace.* And Jake's plea to hear his father out and avoid litigation if possible. But if he gave in now, it would be as if he were a little kid heeding Dad's decree. Still standing, he asked, "So why did you come?''

"I wanted to see you.''

"You saw me in Judge Monsanto's office.''

"And you never even spoke to me.'' His father sounded wounded.

"I didn't know what to say. I couldn't very well have congratulated you on winning, now could I?'' He shook his head in disgust. "That's all you ever care about anyway—winning. It's the most important thing. The *only* thing.''

"No!'' his father said sharply. "This isn't about winning.'' Jeremy saw that tears had sprung to his father's eyes. He waited while his father reined in his emotions. "It's about losing, Jeremy. It's about losing you."

Slowly Jeremy sat down.

His father continued, "I've already lost one son. I can't lose another."

"Tom," Jeremy whispered.

"He was alive. Then in an instant he was dead. Nothing in all my years of living prepared me for that. I only know I can't go through it again."

"I'm not going to die, Dad."

"I know it's an irrational fear," his father said, raking his hand through his hair. "I know that thousands of people undergo surgery every day and come out just fine. I know that in my head. But in my heart—" He shook his head. "I can't stand to think about you dying on the table. Or suffering irreversible damage. Of you ending up like Tom. And if any of those things happened, I would be responsible because I agreed to let you do it. In short, it would be *my* fault if something bad happened to you."

Stunned by the fervor in his father's voice, astounded by the scenario his fears had written,

Jeremy found it difficult to respond. Finally he said, "I'm not Tom."

"That's what the psychiatrist at the hospital told me."

"You spoke to her? When? Why?"

His father rubbed his eyes and let out his breath. "I stormed into her office after you passed all the hospital tests. I went to fight with her, to castigate her for saying a sixteen-year-old boy was competent to make the decision to give away an organ."

"That's what her report said," Jeremy declared. He barely recalled that part of the testing process.

"I didn't think a woman who'd seen you for a couple of hours could know you as well as your own parents. I called her names, I yelled and told her she was a puppet of the hospital, doing their bidding because they wanted to perform another transplant."

"You didn't!" Jeremy cried, appalled.

His father shrugged. "I told her you'd lost a brother—how could you be rational? You know what she said?"

Jeremy shook his head, fascinated by the story.

"She said, 'Mr. Travino, Jeremy's dealt amazingly well with his brother's death. I suspect that's because he's talked about it so much with Jessica and traveled through so many aspects of the grieving process. You, sir, however, haven't even begun to deal with it.'"

Jeremy's jaw dropped. *His father?* He was always so much in control. He was brilliant, tenacious, unflappable. And yet *he* hadn't fully dealt with Tom's death?

"Is it true? How about Mom?"

"I'm afraid she isn't coping with it either. And that's my fault too. I never let her talk about it to me. And I never even guessed how badly she needed to. You brought it all to a head when you packed your bags and walked out."

"But I never meant to hurt you or Mom. I just wanted to help Jessica. I didn't know how else to do it."

For the first time, his father offered a wry smile. "You're too much like me, Jeremy. You even used my own ploy from my college days against me by getting law students to defend you. You settled on a course of action, and you took it. Do you know how hard it's been for me to have to sit back and let other forces control my life? Emancipation . . ." He shook his head. "That took guts. I've been torn between wanting to be proud of you and wanting to choke you."

"You wouldn't listen to anything I had to say and we were running out of time. We still are," Jeremy added.

His father laced his fingers together and stared at Jeremy across the table. Jeremy held his gaze without flinching. At last his father said, "Your mother and I will sign the consent form. We don't want to lose you, son, and if we don't say yes, you'll hate us. Please be part of our family. We need you."

Jeremy leaped to his feet again. "Dad, you'll really sign?"

"Only if you promise not to die on us."

A slow smile spread across Jeremy's face. "You got it."

"So let's call in your attorney and break the news that he's out of work."

Jeremy hurried to the door and yanked it open. A startled Jake, who'd been sitting on a chair near the door, jumped to his feet. "We're dropping the suit!" Jeremy exclaimed. "My parents are going to allow me to donate."

Jake stepped into the room and regarded Jeremy's father cautiously. "Is that true, sir?"

"It's true."

Jake's face broke into a grin. "I think that's great news." He held out his hand, and Frank Travino took it.

"Can I ask you on what grounds you were planning to appeal?" Frank asked. "Just for the record."

"Constitutional grounds."

"Federal court?" Jeremy's father asked, sounding surprised.

"You know—what rights a minor has over his own body," Jake said. "It's a constitutional issue."

"I guess you could plead that," Frank said, looking impressed.

"It was Jeremy's idea."

Frank turned and looked Jeremy full in the face. In his eyes Jeremy could have sworn that he saw astonishment. And pride.

————

The next thing Jeremy did was head for the phone to call Jessica. Her mother answered on the first ring. "Mrs. McMillan—," he started.

"Is Jessica with you?" Her voice sounded high and thin, edgy, near hysteria.

His heart thudded. "No, she's not."

Her mother let out a strangled cry. "Oh, Jeremy, she's missing. She never came home from dialysis today."

Chapter

18

Traffic on U.S. Highway 17 was at a stand-still in both directions and had been for over an hour. Jessica had sat in the car with the engine running until she realized she wasn't going anywhere. She turned off the engine, got out of the car and paced the shoulder of the road with other stranded motorists. She heard them talking about the tie-up.

"A semi overturned."

"According to my CB, it was carrying hazardous chemicals and spilled the stuff over both sides of the road."

"The cleanup could take hours!"

"How far to the next exit?"

"Maybe ten miles."

"Then we're stuck?"

"Guess so."

Jessica climbed back into her car and turned on the air-conditioning for a few minutes. The summer sun was broiling, her head was throbbing and she felt sick to her stomach. She realized too late that her mother had taken the car phone with her in their older, less reliable car so that Jessica could have the newer vehicle. She was out of communication with everyone.

The clock on the dashboard read 3:00 P.M. She also realized the trip to the beach was out. She had to wait until she could get to an exit so that she could turn around and head back to the Washington area. "This is the pits," she mumbled. She laid her head against the back of the seat and shut her eyes.

Jeremy had gone straight to Jessica's house from the campus. Because of daylight saving time, it was still light at seven o'clock, but the fading sun only made him feel more anxious. Her parents were beside themselves with worry. "The dialysis unit said she left at eleven-thirty," her mother said tearfully. "I called the police, but they can't begin an official search until she's been missing longer."

"But she's got medical problems," Jeremy blurted. "And this isn't like her. I'd called to tell you good news. This can't be happening just when it's all going to work out."

Jeremy paced the floor, his heart thudding with fear. Something was wrong. Jessica always came home after dialysis. Often she got sick, and he knew she would want to be in familiar surroundings. "I think I know a way to speed up the police," he said.

"Do it," Ruth pleaded.

Jeremy dialed his home number, telling Jessica's mother, "My father will help."

When traffic finally began to creep forward, Jessica inched along with it, willing her car to the nearest exit. Once there, she'd find a phone and call home. It was just five; her parents wouldn't even be home yet and wouldn't have missed her. She'd leave a message on the answering machine telling them she was on her way and not to worry.

It was almost six when she finally made it to the exit, but it took another twenty minutes to get off the ramp. Traffic at the two gas stations near the exit was backed up for a mile in either direction and the lines for the phone seemed just as long.

She heard one motorist tell another, "Can't return on Seventeen because it's a snarl with everybody trying to get back to Washington. Right now we're just hoping to find a place to spend the night."

Dismayed, she decided to go home by another route. She studied the map, but felt confusion spreading over her like a thick fog. *I should eat something,* she told herself. She found an old granola bar and a bag of pretzels in the glove compartment. She'd worry about her special diet later.

She drove, allowing the air-conditioning to blast in her face. The coolness made her feel better. When she saw a country side road, her heart leaped. Quickly she turned onto it. Surely there'd be a farmhouse somewhere along the old road where she could stop and call home for help.

Jeremy had to hand it to his father. The man certainly had clout and knew how to use it. He and Marilyn had rushed right over when Jeremy called, and after Jeremy's brief reunion with his tearful mother, he watched his father go to work.

Frank called prominent people, barking orders and threats into the phone. By nine o'clock the police had put out an all points bulletin on Jessica's car. "If any officer spots it, we'll know," said the detective who'd come to Jessica's house.

"What if she's been carjacked?" Her mother was nearly hysterical.

"We'll find her," the detective said.

Jeremy's mother tried to comfort Jessica's.

Earlier, while they'd waited, he'd told Don and Ruth about having his parents' consent to donate his kidney. The news fell flat. How could he donate an organ to a girl who was missing? One who could be in serious trouble?

The country road had turned into a trail of rutted red clay and weeds. "Don't panic," Jessica told herself, forcing down waves of fear.

All she had to do was turn around and go back the way she'd come. She'd return to the highway; surely by now the traffic would have cleared. She backed the car over the rough, hard Virginia ground and felt a rear tire sag. The sun was dipping low—soon it would be dark.

Her mouth felt dry as cotton. If only she had a sip of water. *Medications!* With a start, she realized she hadn't taken her evening medicines. At least she had a pill bottle in her purse with a dose of the most vital prescriptions. She looked for a place to stop that was friendlier than the rutted road. It was terribly hot since now the air-conditioning seemed to be blowing hot air and wasn't working properly. She saw a large tree in the middle of a field; it looked cool and inviting. *Maybe if I rest awhile, I'll feel better,* she told herself. Carefully she drove toward the tree, hearing the *thump, thump* of the tire.

Beneath the tree's branches, the air was cooler. Her shoes pinched, and she knew her feet were swollen. Still she got out and limped around to the back of the car and saw that her right rear tire was flat. She didn't have either the strength or expertise to change the tire. She fought down panic. Someone would find her. Sooner or later, she'd be found.

She returned to the car, where she fumbled in her purse until she found the pill bottle. Her mouth was so dry she couldn't swallow, so she said to herself, "I'll take a little nap." Things would look better after some sleep.

Jeremy's father called the local media at ten o'clock, hoping to get a story about Jessica on the late news. Jeremy drove to several local stations with photos of Jessica and a brief description of her medical condition.

A reporter from *The Washington Post* came to the house and did an interview with Jessica's parents, telling them he'd have the story on the front page of the morning edition. He asked, "Was your daughter depressed? I mean, about her condition and all?"

"She was coping," Don McMillan said.

"She wouldn't have simply run off, would she?"

"No!" He sounded angry. "She knows she can't survive without dialysis. Besides, we've just learned that she is to receive a kidney transplant. It's what she's been waiting for."

Jeremy was thankful that Don hadn't looked toward him. At this point he didn't want the press to know *he* was to be Jessica's donor. He didn't want to answer a hundred questions. Didn't want them to know about the lawsuit. It might only add fuel to their speculation on her running away.

At eleven the local news channels ran the story about Jessica along with her photo. At midnight the detective who had remained with them at the house suggested they all go to bed and promised he'd keep them apprised of any new information.

Of course, no one went to bed. Jeremy waited by the phone with both sets of parents, drinking coffee and willing the phone to ring. But it didn't—not once during the long and arduous night.

Jessica awoke with a start. She'd fallen asleep across the seat of the car. The lights on the dashboard had gone out. With a sickening sensation, she realized that she hadn't turned off the key, and the interior lights and radio had run down the battery. Her heart thudded wildly.

She tried to start the engine, but it made a grinding sound and she knew the battery was dead. A flat tire and a dead battery. *Not good,* she thought. She imagined her parents worrying about her. And Jeremy. She'd give anything to see his face, have him hug her. She wondered how his meeting with his father had gone. She hoped she got out of this mess in time to find out.

Outside, the moon drifted from behind the clouds, and in its weak light she squinted at the face of her watch: 3:00 A.M. By now, she hoped, people were out looking for her. The night air was humid, and the dampness made her feel chilled. She mumbled a prayer, curled up in a ball and fell into a fitful sleep.

Jessica's picture and story were all over the morning news shows and papers. A headline read: MISSING GIRL NEEDS DIALYSIS. Jeremy rubbed his eyes, bloodshot from lack of sleep, and read every word. The phone at Jessica's house started ringing as concerned friends and neighbors called. The detective cut the callers short, telling them the line had to be kept open for important police calls, and just in case Jessica called home herself.

Jessica's mother had been given tranquilizers, so she slept. When Jessica's father felt heart palpitations, his doctor insisted on bed rest or immediate hospitalization. Don McMillan chose to remain in bed. Jeremy's parents became responsible for cooking, fending off reporters, doing whatever needed to be done. He himself was torn between going to look for her and staying close to the phone in case she was found. One call that got through in the late afternoon was from Dr. Witherspoon. "This isn't good," the doctor told Jeremy. "She probably doesn't have her medications with her."

Jeremy could confirm that. The bottles stood upstairs on her dresser. He told the doctor that his parents had relented and that when Jessica was found, he could donate his kidney to her.

"Let's just hope she's found in time," Dr. Witherspoon said grimly. "She needs to be stable for the surgery. And you'll need to be prepped for it too."

In a trembling voice, Jeremy asked, "How long can she go without dialysis?"

"Maybe a week," Dr. Witherspoon said.

It had already been over twenty-four hours since she'd left the dialysis unit.

"We've *got* to find her soon."

Chapter

19

Jessica woke when the sun slanted into her eyes. She felt hot and sticky all over. She groaned as she tried to sit upright. For a few dazed moments, she attempted to figure out where she was; then, in a jumble of memories, it came back to her. She was stranded in a field out in the middle of nowhere.

She thought about walking up the road, but quickly realized she hadn't the strength. *What day is it?* Her head was in a fog and her skin itched like crazy. She needed dialysis. She was panting, and it hurt to breathe deeply. "Jeremy," she called weakly.

Why didn't he come for her? Why was he

staying away? "I need you, Jeremy. I need you."

"It's been four days," Jeremy wailed to the detective. "Four days! You should have found her by now."

"You're assuming she wants to be found," the man countered.

"Of course she wants to be found. What kind of idea is that? She's somewhere suffering from uremia. She can't get to a phone. She's probably hurt. Her doctor says she may be in a coma someplace."

The detective put a hand on Jeremy's shoulder. "I don't need you to freak out on me, son. Stay calm. Every clue, every lead is being followed up. It takes time."

"She doesn't have any time." Jeremy felt desperate, crazy with worry. Jessica's time was running out.

In her dreams, she drifted in a sea of lapping water. If she came too close to the surface, she hurt. It was as if her body were on fire. *Thirsty. So thirsty.* All she had to do was turn her head and lap the cool water, but when she tried, the water receded and the pain was excruciating.

She was hot. She was cold. She thought another day and night passed, but she wasn't sure. She wondered if she was dying. *Poor Jessica,* she heard imaginary voices say. *Poor, poor Jessica. She drowned on the way to the beach in a field of grass in a car that would not start.*

"It's the first break we've had," the detective told them with a tremor of excitement.

The news about Jessica had become a national story. Calls came in from all over about supposed sightings of her car. Jeremy's father said, "We've heard from people as far away as California. How do you know this one is the real thing?"

Jeremy listened with mounting excitement as the detective said, "A woman called who'd been stranded on U.S. Seventeen by that overturned tanker truck five days ago. She remembered a girl who looked like Jessica standing on the shoulder of the road near her. She described the clothes Jessica was wearing exactly, and we haven't released all those details to the press."

"U.S. Seventeen," Jessica's mother said, confused. "What was she doing out that way?"

"No idea," the detective said. "But at least we can concentrate our search in that area."

Jeremy called Dr. Witherspoon with the news. "The minute they find her, you call the hospital," the doctor said. "We'll send the Life Force Helicopter for her. And you get here fast too. We'll do the transplant just as soon as she's stable."

For the first time in days, Jeremy dared to hope they might find Jessica in time.

She heard a dog barking. The sound came from far, far away. She wanted the animal to hush. Didn't it know she was trying to sleep? A gray fog shrouded her now, beckoning her ever deeper into its depths. She wanted to slip inside its soft gray arms and find peace, but something kept her from going.

She vaguely heard a pounding sound. And a voice. "Wake up, girlie! Unlock the door. Wake up."

She couldn't move.

She heard a noise—glass cracking? She felt the wet, cold nose of a dog and a man's hands lifting her. And a voice saying, "I got you, girlie. Don't you worry. Old Luther's got you."

"An old man going fishing found her in a field. Her car had a flat tire and a dead battery." The detective relayed the information to Jeremy and both sets of parents. "An ambulance is taking her to the nearest hospital—it's just a small community facility. I'll dispatch the helicopter from here."

"How is she?" Jessica's mother's voice trembled.

Jeremy held his breath, waiting for the answer.

"She's alive. But not by much."

Jeremy gazed at Jessica through the window of the intensive care unit, hardly recognizing her. Tubes and wires seemed to be growing out of her body. She was swollen with water weight, and her skin had a ghastly greenish tinge.

"Are you all right, son?"

He turned to see his father, who'd come up beside him. "I'm all right, Dad," he said pensively, "nobody should have to die of kidney failure. It's a terrible way to die."

"I never had an appreciation of dialysis the way I do now. Seeing her like this . . ." Frank didn't complete his thought.

"And nobody should have to live their life hooked to a machine if they can get a transplant. That's why I know I'm doing the right thing by giving her my kidney."

"I'm still afraid for you."

"I'm going to be fine."

"Dr. Witherspoon says the incision on your back to remove your kidney will be about fifteen inches." He held out his hands to demonstrate the length for Jeremy. "You'll have a scar there all your life."

"Jessica will have one too," Jeremy countered.

"Your recovery won't be easy."

"Hers will take longer."

"Nothing I can say will dissuade you, will it?"

"Nothing."

His father sighed. "I didn't think so. You've already missed the start of school, you know."

"It won't be a problem." He'd already decided to finish his senior year. The schoolwork was easy for him. It would give him more time to be with Jessica while she recovered and adjusted to her new kidney and antirejection medications.

"I'll be glad when this is all behind us," his father commented.

"Me too."

"Just for the record"—his father gripped his shoulder—"I'm proud to call you my son."

His father left, and Jeremy turned to gaze once again at Jessica as she slept. He pressed his forehead against the glass partition and said a prayer of thanks to God for sparing her. Then, for the first time since the ordeal had begun, Jeremy allowed himself to cry.

After she left intensive care for a private room, Jessica learned that she'd become a minicelebrity. "You mean I was on national news?"

"Yes," her mother said. "The mail still hasn't stopped coming."

"And your room looks like a florist shop," her father added.

Jessica felt embarrassed.

"We saved all the newspaper clippings for you to read," Jeremy added.

"I would have rather become famous some other way," she admitted. "It was so weird when I was stuck out in that field. I wanted to do something to help myself, but I couldn't. My brain felt fogged in."

"It's just as well," her father said. "The police said the smartest thing you did was to stay with the car. If you'd tried to walk away and collapsed—"

"Well, it's over." She interrupted him. "And now the real work begins." She looked up at Jeremy. "Dr. Witherspoon told me the transplant is set for day after tomorrow. You sure you don't want to change your mind?"

"What? And miss my chance to make the national news?" he kidded. "Maybe they'll want to make a TV minimovie about us."

She rolled her eyes.

"They could get a hot young star to play me. And who could they pick to play you?" he mused.

"Willy the Whale?"

He chuckled, then sobered. "No matter how this turns out, Jessie, I don't have any regrets."

Two days later their beds stood side by side in the preop room as they waited for the transplant teams to assemble. Jeremy would be in one operating room and Jessica in another. One team of surgeons would snip out his healthy kidney and sew him up, and the other team would place the organ in Jessica's body. The whole procedure would take four to five hours.

Jeremy felt as if he were floating. "This stuff they gave me to relax sure does work," he told Jessica.

She wore a green cap over her hair and had an IV line attached to the back of her hand. "Do I look as silly as you?" Her speech was slurred.

"You think I look silly? I'm wounded." But he couldn't suppress a grin.

"Just as soon as you're able to move, you come visit me," she said.

"I'll be there."

Two anesthesiologists appeared. "Time to go to sleep." They injected medications into Jeremy's and Jessica's IV lines.

Dr. Witherspoon leaned over their beds and smiled. "Okay, you two. It's showtime."

Jeremy felt the medication numbing his

body. He turned his head and saw that Jessica was staring at him, her eyelids heavy with the drugs. He reached his hand through the bars of the bed. She laced her fingers through his. "I love you, Jessie."

Moisture filled her eyes. "Thank you, Jeremy. Thank you for my new life."

Chapter
20

"You look beautiful."

Jessica smiled. "Thanks for the compliment, but you're prejudiced. After all, we share body parts."

She gazed around the ballroom of the hotel, at the girls in beautiful dresses and gowns, at the boys in formal tuxedos.

"I must admit I feel funny out here," she whispered in his ear. "I'll bet I'm the only college freshman at this high-school prom."

"You missed yours. I thought you should come to mine. Aren't you glad you're here with me?"

She slid her arms around him and knew that beneath his tux, along his back, was the scar that attested to his gift to her. There had been a few problems after her transplant, but for the most part it had been trouble-free. She took antirejection medication, and her body appeared to have accepted his kidney.

"One of my friends is having a weekender on his grandfather's boat after the prom. The boat's anchored in the harbor at Annapolis," Jeremy said.

"I hope there'll be food."

He grinned. "A crate of lobsters and a mountain of french fries."

"Count me in."

Jeremy hugged her tightly. She looked sophisticated in a long black dress that clung to her shapely body. Her thick hair had been swept into a luxurious twist and her eyes sparkled with vitality. Jeremy thought she looked far more elegant than the high-school girls around them on the dance floor.

"I'm so glad that I'll be going to Georgetown in the fall," he said.

"I've been hoping that would be your choice."

"Okay, so the fact that you're there influenced me a tiny bit. I've also decided to go into their prelaw program. It's one of the best."

"Why doesn't it surprise me?" she teased.

He shrugged sheepishly. "I'm told I have a flare for it. My dad says, 'like father like son.' I have to admit, it's great to see what's happened to my parents. The group they joined, Compassionate Friends, has helped them meet other parents whose children have died. They're happier than I've seen them in years."

"I'm glad you and your family didn't split apart because of me," Jessica said slowly.

"Listen, Jake and Fran both passed their bar exams and found jobs." Jeremy changed the subject quickly. "Jake was like a brother to me." His voice cracked as he said "brother."

"Did I tell you what I'm considering? I think I want to major in biology and become a premed."

Jeremy laughed and kissed her lightly on her mouth. "Wait'll I tell my mom. She's always wanted a doctor in the family."

Jessica kissed him back, knowing that no matter what happened their lives were intertwined forever.

Look for Lurlene McDaniel's next book,

I'll Be Seeing You

When a chemistry experiment explodes, seventeen-year-old Kyle is left blinded and deeply depressed. As he is recovering in the hospital, he is befriended by Carley, a patient in the room next door. Carley becomes Kyle's eyes and his cheerleader, giving him hope and a link to the outside world.

Carley has never met a boy as handsome as Kyle. She knows that boys like girls who are pretty—and she is not. Scarred by a facial deformity that no plastic surgeon can fix, she has, over the years, used her sense of humor to cope. But now that she's become so close to Kyle, she's worried that once his bandages are removed—*if* they are removed—and he sees her, it will be the end of their relationship. Carley wants the best for Kyle—but what will that mean for her?

LURLENE McDANIEL began writing inspirational novels about teenagers facing life-altering situations when her son was diagnosed with juvenile diabetes. "I saw firsthand how chronic illness affects every aspect of a person's life," she has said. "I want kids to know that while people don't get to choose what life gives to them, they *do* get to choose how they respond."

Lurlene McDaniel's novels are hard-hitting and realistic, but also leave readers with inspiration and hope. Her books have received acclaim from readers, teachers, parents, and reviewers. *Six Months to Live* was included in a literary time capsule at the Library of Congress in Washington, D.C. Lurlene McDaniel lives in Chattanooga, Tennessee.

Her popular Bantam Starfire books include *Too Young to Die; Goodbye Doesn't Mean Forever; Somewhere Between Life and Death; Time to Let Go; Now I Lay Me Down to Sleep; When Happily Ever After Ends; Baby Alicia Is Dying; Don't Die, My Love;* and the One Last Wish novels: *A Time to Die; Mourning Song; Mother, Help Me Live; Someone Dies, Someone Lives; Sixteen and Dying; Let Him Live; The Legacy: Making Wishes Come True; Please Don't Die; She Died Too Young; All the Days of Her Life;* and *A Season for Goodbye.*